My Father, the
Angel of Death

My Father, the Angel of Death

Ray Villareal

PIÑATA
BOOKS

PIÑATA BOOKS
ARTE PÚBLICO PRESS
HOUSTON, TEXAS

This volume is funded in part by grants from the City of Houston through The Cultural Arts Council of Houston/Harris County and by the Exemplar Program, a program of Americans for the Arts in Collaboration with the LarsonAllen Public Services Group, funded by the Ford Foundation.

Piñata Books are full of surprises!

Piñata Books

An imprint of
Arte Público Press
University of Houston
452 Cullen Performance Hall
Houston, Texas 77204-2004

Illustration by Alejandro Romero
Cover design by Giovanni Mora & Gianni Mora

Villareal, Ray.
 My Father, the Angel of Death / by Ray Villareal.
  p. cm.
 Summary: Seventh-grader Jesse Baron not only misses his father, a popular professional wrestler who is often on the road, he faces simple family outings that turn into fan-frenzy events, teachers who contrive excuses for parent-teacher conferences, and friendships that are all suspect.
 ISBN: 978-1-55885-466-6
 [1. Wrestling—Fiction. 2. Fathers and sons—Fiction.
3. Celebrities—Fiction. 4. Fame—Fiction. 5. Schools—Fiction.
6. San Antonio (Tex.)—Fiction.] I. Title.
PZ7.V718My 2006
[Fic]—dc22
                                                      2006043241
                                                             CPI

7 8 9 0 1 2 3 4 5 6   10 9 8 7 6 5 4 3 2

For Sylvia, Mateo, and Ana

&

To the memory of my father, Fermin Villareal,
who inspired me to write.

The lyrics to *La dueña de mi amor* are from a poem my father wrote for my mother in 1932, while they were dating.

The bright lights dimmed, leaving the coliseum bathed in an eerie, bluish glow. Strained organ chords filled the air with a haunting, discordant tune.

Suddenly, a powerful, deafening explosion rattled the walls. Streams of orange and yellow flames shot upward in tall columns, and a cloud of smoke billowed from the mouth of the arena.

The spectators, frenzied with anticipation, immediately leaped to their feet.

"Death! Death! Death! Death!" they chanted in unison. "Death! Death! Death! Death!"

Then, as in reply to their cries, a gigantic, ominous figure, dressed in black, emerged from the swirling haze. His long, wispy, dark hair hung loosely around his white, skeleton face. A hooded cloak was draped around his massive frame. In his hand, he clutched a wood-handled scythe with a razor-sharp blade.

His presence electrified the crowd.

"Death! Death! Death! Death!"

The man in black paused. He gazed up at the hordes of people that surrounded him. His piercing eyes widened. Raising his scythe in the air, he unleashed a banshee-like scream.

"Aaagghh!"

The crowd was ecstatic. "Death! Death! Death! Death!"

With slow, but deliberate strides, he made his way to the ring.

His opponent, a man named Raven Starr, fearfully waited for him there, like a condemned prisoner facing a firing squad.

The man in black climbed through the ropes. He removed his cloak and handed it and the scythe to a waiting attendant. Then he stepped to the center of the ring, stopping inches away from Raven Starr. He stood rigid, like a statue. His coal-black eyes bore deeply into Starr's. Within moments, Raven Starr's eyes became blank, mesmerized by the man in black's intense, hypnotic stare.

All at once, without warning, the man in black struck! He sprang back with a short step. Then he lunged forward, assaulting Starr with a devastating clothesline that knocked him senselessly down to the mat.

The crowd screamed wildly in approval. "Death! Death! Death! Death!"

The man in black responded by pounding his chest like an enraged gorilla.

"Aaagghh!"

Raven Starr sluggishly rolled over on all fours. He gave his head a quick shake to regain his senses. He staggered to his feet and readied himself for another wave of attack.

The man in black charged forward. This time, Starr fired back with a short series of punches. But they were about as effective as a rabbit fending off a lion.

The man in black, his face a grinning skull, laughed maniacally at Starr's efforts. He forced him into a corner and pummeled Starr relentlessly with jackhammer punches. Raven Starr's body crumpled to the floor.

The man in black lifted him like a rag doll, and with incredible force, power-bombed him onto the mat.

"Aaagghh!" he roared, thrusting his arms victoriously in the air.

"Death! Death! Death! Death!" cried the crowd, now gesturing a "thumbs down."

Having accepted the people's verdict, the man in black grabbed his victim, flipped him upside down, and delivered the final blow, the coup de grace, the Death Drop Pile Driver.

"THE WINNER OF THE MATCH . . . AND STILL . . . THE ACW HEAVYWEIGHT CHAMPION," the ring announcer bellowed, *"THE AAANGEL OF DEAAATH!"*

Thunderous applause and cheers echoed throughout the arena. "Death! Death! Death! Death!"

Once again, the blue lights blanketed the room and the unharmonious organ music sounded. The man in black exited the ring and marched triumphantly up the aisle.

Despite the seemingly vicious onslaught I had just witnessed, I smiled. I knew Raven Starr would be all right. He always was.

The man in black disappeared into the enveloping fog, withdrawing to the lower regions of the Netherworld, where he would wait until the Dark Forces summoned him once more.

There he goes, I thought, as I watched him leave. *My father . . . the Angel of Death.*

CHAPTER ONE

Thump-thump! Thump-thump! Thump-thump! Thump-thump!

The kettledrums pounded unmercifully inside my head. I pressed my fingers against my temples to try to ease the pain, but it didn't do any good.

Thump-thump! Thump-thump! Thump-thump! Thump-thump!

If only I had an aspirin or something I could take to get rid of this excruciating headache. I knew there'd be no point in asking the school nurse for one. The best she could offer was a few minutes' rest on one of the cots in the clinic. I learned that on my first day of school when I asked for permission to see the nurse, after developing another one of my now, all too frequently occurring headaches.

"Hey, Jesse, wait up!" a voice called from behind me.

Oh, no, Wendell, I thought. *Please, not right now.*

A moment later Wendell Cooley bounded up to me, gasping for air, even though he couldn't have run more than a few yards. I don't know how much Wendell weighed, but I would estimate that he was closing in on three hundred pounds.

"I watched your dad on TV last night," he said excitedly. "He was awesome!" Wendell took a couple of breaths to steady himself. "I can hardly wait 'til he fights

Prince Romulus at the pay-per-view. That's gonna be the best match on the card."

"Yeah, I guess," I said with a shrug. I hoped Wendell would take the hint that I didn't feel like talking about it.

"You must be the luckiest kid in the world to have the Angel of Death for a father," Wendell gushed.

Instantly my headache skipped up to the next level of pain.

Thump-thump! Thump-thump! Thump-thump! Thump-THUMP!

My head felt as if it was going to split open, like a watermelon dropped on the sidewalk.

"Look, Wendell," I said as politely as I could. "I don't feel too well right now, okay?"

Wendell looked at me with concern. Then his mouth stretched into a wide, 'possum grin. "Oh, yeah, I know what you mean. I'll bet you didn't have a lot of time to study for the Texas history test, did you? Tell you the truth, neither did I." He patted me on the back with a chubby hand. "But I wasn't about to miss *Monday Night Mayhem* to study for a stupid test, that's for sure. Anyway, I know we'll both do just fine."

We continued walking to school with Wendell jabbering about last night's matches. The pain-driven drumbeats in my head drowned out most of everything he said. If only I could get rid of this maddening headache—it, and Wendell Cooley.

Wendell paused to catch his breath after rattling off something about why Wally Armstrong was still wrestling, even though he hadn't won a match in over three months.

"Um, listen, Jesse," he said. "Me and Terrance and Goose and some of the other guys were wondering if we could come over to your house some time. You know, to meet your dad and get his autograph and stuff."

Here it comes, I thought. The same thing as in Omaha, Atlanta, Tampa, St. Louis, and just about every other city in between. How long had we been in San Antonio? A week, going on two?

When we first moved here, I decided, from past experience, not to let anyone know who my father was. At least not right away. Not until the kids got to know me first. I knew what their reaction would be. I'd gone through it plenty of times. So I wasn't the one who blabbed it out to the whole class. No, that honor went to my new seventh grade homeroom teacher, Mrs. Petrosky.

"It appears that we have the son of a famous celebrity in our class," my teacher announced on my first day at Sidney Lanier Middle School. "Would anyone like to guess who Jesse Baron's father is?"

"The Red Baron?" a kid shouted from the back of the room. The class laughed.

Mrs. Petrosky ignored him. She glanced down at the pink enrollment form in her hand. Then with a grin on her face that would've made the Cheshire Cat envious, she blurted out, "Jesse's father is the American Championship Wrestling Heavyweight Champion, the Angel of Death!"

For a second the whole class fell silent, as if someone had aimed a remote control at them and pressed the MUTE button. The next moment, they exploded with skeptical jeers and laughter. Perhaps they thought Mrs. Petrosky was playing an early joke on them, since April Fool's Day was coming up that Friday.

"I'm serious," she said, still smiling. "Jesse's father is Mark Baron, otherwise known in professional wrestling as the Angel of Death. They've just moved here from St. Louis."

She turned and gazed dreamily at me, her grin still pasted firmly on her face. Apparently she was a wrestling fan. I didn't realize until later just how big a fan she really was.

"Maybe you'd like to share with us what it's like to be the son of a wrestling superstar, Jesse," she said.

Thump-thump! Thump-thump! Thump-thump! Thump-thump!

I stared at the sea of strange faces in the room, anxiously waiting for me to say something. My palms got sweaty. My legs felt like spaghetti. The class became one gigantic blur.

Thump-thump! Thump-thump! Thump-thump! Thump-thump!

"I-I don't feel . . . I mean . . . my head hurts, ma'am," I muttered. "It hurts a lot." I looked up at her with pleading eyes.

Mrs. Petrosky's smile melted.

"Well," she said with obvious disappointment. "I'm sure you're a little nervous, with this being your first day and everything. Let's find you a seat, and later, after you feel a little better, maybe you can tell us all about your amazing father."

She led me to a desk next to the fattest seventh grader I'd ever seen. As I sat down, the fat kid smiled proudly, like he'd just won the drawing for the Grand Prize at the Jesse Baron Giveaway Contest.

Thump-thump! Thump-thump! Thump-thump! Thump-thump!

"So, what do you think, Jesse?" Wendell asked hopefully. "Is it okay if we come over?"

I shrugged and mumbled, "I don't know."

"We wouldn't take up a lot of your dad's time," Wendell persisted. "We just want to see the Angel of Death up close. You know, in person."

"I understand, Wendell, it's just that . . . "

Thump-thump! Thump-thump! Thump-thump! Thump-thump!

"I'm never really sure when my father's going to be home."

By the expression on Wendell's face, I'm sure he thought I was trying to brush him off. To a certain extent, I was. Still, I wasn't making that part up. I lowered my eyes and squeezed the sides of my head tightly, but the pain refused to go away.

"Well, well, well. If it ain't the Angel of Dorks and his fat sidekick, El Blubber."

I glanced up and saw Manny Alvarez and his goons, Chester Leonard and Hugo Sanchez, approaching us.

"I watched your old man wrestle yesterday," Manny said with a sneer. "What a joke! The only reason the ACW puts him up against jobbers like Raven Starr is 'cause everyone knows the Angel of Death can't carry a full match anymore. Not against the top talent, anyway. Guys like Ice Man Jacob Sloane and Bronko Savage would easily expose him for the washed up has-been he is."

Wendell glared indignantly at them. "He's fighting Prince Romulus at *The Final Stand* in two weeks, isn't he?" he said, coming to my father's defense.

"Shut your pie hole, *panzón*, before I shut it for you," Manny threatened. Chester and Hugo giggled like a couple of first grade girls. "Romulus is a mid-carder at best.

He doesn't have any business even fighting for the heavy-weight title. Anyway," Manny continued, "the only reason to order *The Final Stand* is to watch Ice Man Sloane against Butcher Murdock in the Steel Cage Match. Nobody wants to watch The Angel of Dead Meat wrestle anymore."

Manny paused and waited for my reaction, but I didn't respond. I didn't want to say anything to provoke him any further. For whatever reason, he'd disliked me from the beginning.

On April Fool's Day, he and Chester and Hugo burst into the classroom that morning and frantically announced that they'd just heard on the news that the Angel of Death and several other wrestlers had been killed in a car crash outside of Denver. My father had wrestled a "house show" there the night before, and I hadn't heard from him since he'd left for his match.

There was a collective gasp of horror from everyone. My eyes flooded with tears, and my heart dropped down to my toes.

Suddenly Manny exclaimed, "April Fool!"

Chester and Hugo howled with laughter.

Mrs. Petrosky, who had been nearly as devastated as I was at their shocking announcement, angrily scolded them. Then she lectured the class about playing sick jokes.

"The wrestling web sites on the Internet say your dad's knees are shot," said Manny. "That's why the ACW doesn't match him up against the faster wrestlers like Kid Dynamo or Red Lassiter. Is that true?" His voice softened with what seemed genuine concern.

Can you believe this guy? After ripping into my father, Manny thought I'd be all too happy to share some inside information with him that the Internet fans only speculated about.

"My father's knees are fine," I said coldly.

Thump-thump! Thump-thump! Thump-thump! Thump-thump!

I lowered my head, grimacing in pain.

"Look, I think he's gonna cry," I heard Chester say in a singsong voice.

"You hurt his feelings talking about his daddy that way," added Hugo. "Boo, hoo, hoo." He balled up his hands and pretended to rub his eyes.

Manny Alvarez chuckled. "Your old man doesn't deserve to hold the heavyweight belt." His voice changed back to its mocking tone. "If the head honchos at the ACW ever listen to what the fans *really* want, they'll strip him of it and give it to a better, more worthy wrestler."

He shoved Wendell out of the way and headed toward the school blacktop. Chester and Hugo strutted behind him like a couple of obedient poodles.

We stood silently watching them for a few seconds. Finally Wendell rested a fat hand on my shoulder. "I don't care what Manny or anyone else says. The Angel of Death is the coolest wrestler in the whole ACW. He's still the champ, right? The greatest champion of all time, if you ask me."

I suppose his comments were meant to make me feel better. They didn't.

CHAPTER TWO

"But Mark, you promised me you wouldn't work the house show today. You said you were flying home this morning after last night's TV tapings."

"I know, Molly, but Frank Collins dropped this on us at the last minute. He's worried about the potential low buy rates for *The Final Stand*. Frank wants the top-tier wrestlers to work all the house shows between now and then to help generate sales."

"All the house shows? So when are you planning to come home?"

"I don't know. Soon."

"Wednesday? Thursday?"

"Maybe Friday night after the show in Birmingham."

"Friday? Mark, you assured me that things were going to be different once we moved to San Antonio. So tell me how they're different, Mark, would you? How are things different?"

"Please believe me, Molly. There's nothing I can do about it. Listen, why don't you take Jesse to see my folks? After all, that's one of the reasons we moved back to San Antonio, so Jesse could get to know his grandparents better."

"He needs to get to know his father better!"

"I'm sorry, honey, I really am. I've got good news, though. I spoke to Frank about taking some time off after the pay-per-view. He's agreed to give me a four-week break. I'll be able to spend more time with you and Jesse then. I promise, okay?"

"Sure, why not? What's one more broken promise?"

"Try to understand my situation, Molly."

"I understand perfectly, Mark. Being the Angel of Death means more to you than being a husband and a father."

"Molly . . . "

"I know it's not nearly as exciting tossing the football with Jesse as it is having millions of kids begging for your autograph."

"Molly . . . "

"And how can I possibly compete with the thousands of beautiful women who shamelessly throw themselves at you, wanting to touch you, to kiss you?"

"Molly, that's not fair!"

"And what about Spirit? You said she was leaving the company. Why is she still there?"

"Spirit? What does she have to do with . . . ?"

Click!

I sketched a pair of sunglasses on Davy Crockett's face. Then I added a pencil-thin moustache and a goatee. Davy Crockett now sort of resembled one of my father's early tag-team partners, Wild Bill Bronson.

Reading the history test questions for the third time, I kept hoping the answers would somehow surface from the back of my brain, but I was still drawing a blank. Even with my headache gone, I couldn't concentrate hard enough to remember what Mrs. Petrosky had talked about. How did she expect me to know all this stuff about the Texas Revolution, anyway? I'd only been here a little over a week.

I glanced up at her. She sat at her desk, flipping through her teachers' manual. She was sipping a Diet Coke and munching on some Oreo cookies.

Question number one: *Why is Stephen F. Austin called "The Father of Texas?"*

Stephen F. Austin? The only Steve Austin I knew of was the wrestler "Stone Cold" Steve Austin. Over the years I'd heard the fans call him lots of things, but I didn't recall "Father of Texas" being one of them.

I skipped down to the fourth question and changed my answer. It suddenly hit me that it was William B. Travis and not Sam Houston who was the commander at the Alamo. I was on a roll now. Six answers down, only nineteen more to go.

The Alamo was one of those places my father promised he'd take me to visit when we first moved here. So far, he hadn't been home long enough to take me out to buy a hamburger.

When he called this morning to tell my mom not to meet him at the airport, I was afraid she was going to leave him again, like she did a few months ago.

Last July, right before my father left for Chicago to wrestle at the pay-per-view event, *Summer Showdown*, he and my mom got into a heated argument. I'm not exactly sure what it was about, but I figured it was the same stuff they'd been fighting about for the past couple of years. She refused to drive him to the airport.

Before he returned home, my mom packed most of our clothes, and we moved out of our house. She checked us into a Holiday Inn.

Later, when my father came by and tried to talk to her, their discussion escalated to a loud quarrel, with both of them exchanging harsh words and accusations.

After that, my mom and I moved into a small apartment.

Every time the phone rang, she checked the caller ID. If it was my father, she let the answering machine take a message. For a while, the only time I got to see him was when he appeared on *Monday Night Mayhem* on TV.

Finally, on New Year's Day, my parents reconciled.

"To a new beginning," my father toasted. The three of us clanged our champagne glasses together. Actually, my parents had the champagne. I had Seven-Up.

It was then that my father first suggested that we move to Texas.

Question number nine: *Explain the events that led to the Goliad Massacre.*

The Goliad Massacre.

That sounded like a possible name for an ACW pay-per-view show.

The Angel of Death faces Ice Man Jacob Sloane in a "Texas Death Match" at the pay-per-view event of the year, The Goliad Massacre. Call your local cable company and order it now. Whatever you do, don't miss . . . The Goliad Massacre!

I felt like I'd been part of a massacre at home this morning.

My mom had gotten up unusually early. At five thirty, she and the Beatles woke me up with the song "A Hard Day's Night."

Half asleep, I rolled over and glanced at my digital clock. It was still another two and a half hours before I had to report to school.

With my pillow over my head, I tried to block out the noise, but she had her radio on at full blast. So I lay there in the dark, no longer able to go back to sleep. A collage of thoughts and half dreams lazily swam through my head.

Finally, about an hour later, there was a knock at my door. My mom stepped inside and switched on the light.

"Rise and shine, kiddo," she sang. "Time to get ready for school."

"Ahh, you're blinding me!" I cried, throwing my blanket over my face. Then it dawned on me what I had just seen. I brought the blanket back down and gazed up at my mom. She was wearing the sleeveless, shiny-blue dress she'd bought for Aunt Gracie's wedding. Her long, dark-brown hair hung in waves around her shoulders. The air in my room was swallowed up by the strong scent of her perfume.

"Whoa, Mom," I said. "What are you doing dressed up like that? Did Hollywood call?"

"Even better," she replied coyly. "I'm picking Dad up at the airport in a little while."

That didn't make any sense. Normally, whenever she went to meet him, she usually wore jeans and a simple top.

"What happened? Did they toughen the dress code at the airport?" I joked.

My mom glanced at her reflection in my dresser mirror. She rubbed her lips together to spread her lipstick more evenly. "Your father doesn't know it yet, but I'm taking him out for breakfast at this terrific restaurant I discovered at the Riverwalk. Afterwards, we're going shopping. He needs new suits."

I sat up on my bed. "What's the occasion?" I asked. "It's not your anniversary, is it? Because I know it's not his birthday."

She collected my dirty clothes from the floor and tossed them into the hamper. "Nothing special, sweetheart. I just thought I'd surprise him, let him know how much I love him."

Love is not exactly the word I'd use to describe how she felt about him after their phone conversation a short while later.

I showered, got dressed, and made my way to the kitchen. My mom served me a plate of scrambled eggs and a glass of orange juice. She was heating up a flour tortilla when the phone rang.

After she hung up, she sat silently next to me. Her eyes welled up with tears. I felt awkward, not knowing whether I should say anything.

Then I spotted smoke coming from the stove. "Mom, I think the tortilla's burning," I said.

But her mind was miles away. She sat there staring, stone-faced, at the wall. Her lips tightened into an angry, straight line. Her eyes, still filled with tears, widened with rage. I could only imagine the thoughts that were running through her head.

"D-Don't worry, I'll get it," I nervously offered. As I rose from my chair, I accidentally bumped my orange juice glass with my arm. It fell off the table and spilled onto her lap.

"Ay!" she screamed, bolting from her chair. The glass slid off her lap and hit the ceramic tile floor. It shattered into a million pieces. She leaped away from the splattering shards. The juice formed a dark blue stain on her dress and more of it dripped down her legs. She gave her dress a few quick swipes with her hand. "Why don't you watch what you're doing!"

"I–I'm sorry, Mom. I didn't see the glass."

I grabbed a dishtowel from the kitchen island and handed it to her.

She snatched it gruffly from me and dabbed her dress with it. "Do you have any idea how much this dress cost? And now look at it! You've completely ruined it!" She burst into heavy sobs.

"I–I'm sorry, Mom, I really am. It was an accident," I said, but she wasn't listening.

Behind her I saw that the top of the stove was completely engulfed in smoke.

"Mom!" I cried. "The tortilla's on fire!"

She spun around. We both rushed to the stove, colliding into each other.

"Get out of my way!" she yelled.

Without hesitation, I jumped back.

My mom lifted the charred, smoldering mess from the griddle, burning her fingers. She jerked her hand back, dropping the tortilla on the floor. Then she spewed out a string of words I'd never heard come from her mouth. The kinds of words I'm used to hearing from wrestling fans at the arenas whenever they don't like a particular wrestler, but not from my mom.

When she was done, she stood by the stove, crying. She stuffed her fingers in her mouth and tried to suck away the pain. Her mascara streaked down her face like spiderwebs.

I stooped down to pick up the tortilla from the floor.

"Leave it there!" she snapped.

"Why?" I asked.

"Because I said so!"

"I–I'll clear the table then."

"No! Just . . . just go to school." She waved the back of her hand across her face, as if doing so would make the whole incident vanish.

"But I don't have to be in class for another hour," I said against my better judgment.

My mom glared at me. "Get out of this house, Jesse!" she shrieked. "Get out of here now!"

Her screams automatically triggered my headache, but I didn't dare say anything about it. Instead I slowly dragged myself out of the house.

I read through the rest of the questions one more time before deciding there was nothing else I could add to my paper.

This test was impossible. Certainly Mrs. Petrosky would give me a break since I'd been here such a short time.

I turned and stared at Wendell Cooley. He glanced up from his test, grinned, and gave me a "thumbs up."

Wendell really wasn't so bad. He was only trying to be friendly. Still, I couldn't help wonder how chummy he and the other guys would be toward me if my father was Mark Baron, shoe salesman or Mark Baron, construction worker.

A few minutes later, the bell rang. My test paper looked pretty pathetic. But then, I suppose it only reflected how my whole morning had gone so far.

CHAPTER THREE

At lunchtime my new "friends" swarmed my table. Wendell led the pack, followed by Terrance Colby, Abel "Goose" Guzman, and a bunch of other guys whose names I didn't know. As usual, the conversation centered on wrestling.

"What do you want to bet that Kronos is gonna win the Mask vs. Mask match?" Wendell asked the crowd. From what I'd gathered, next to the Angel of Death, Kronos was Wendell's favorite wrestler. "He nearly yanked Black Mamba's mask off the last time they fought," Wendell continued. "And at *The Final Stand*, I'll bet you we're gonna see what Mamba really looks like."

Goose slurped a deep drink of milk from his straw. Then he let out a vicious burp. "No way, Wendy. As soon as Black Mamba clamps the Mamba Stinger on Kronos, it'll be lights out for him. Then Mamba will easily tear off his mask."

"Quit calling me Wendy!" said Wendell, crossly. "And watch your manners, Goose. You act like you don't have any home training."

"Lighten up, Wendy. You call me Goose, and you don't hear me crying about it." Goose burped again.

"No one has to pull anybody's mask off," Terrance broke in. "The loser of the match *has* to remove his mask. That's the stipulation, right, Jesse?"

He asked me as if somehow I was an authority on Mask vs. Mask matches.

"Yeah, I guess," I said flatly.

This discussion was pointless to me since I already knew who was going to "win" the match. Although I held my tongue, Wendell was in for a big disappointment. At *The Final Stand*, it was Kronos whose face was going to be exposed.

A few weeks ago, Kronos began complaining to Frank Collins, the ACW bookmaker and promoter, about an awful rash on his face. He told Mr. Collins that, according to his doctor, the combination of perspiration, the heat, and the fabric of his mask were causing the thick red welts on his skin. His doctor had advised him to wrestle without it.

Mr. Collins understood and assured Kronos, whose real name is Herman Berkowitz, that as soon as he came up with a new gimmick for him, he could get rid of the mask.

A couple of days after that, he approached Kronos with an idea.

"I've got it, Herman," Mr. Collins said. "Listen, after *The Final Stand*, you'll be known as Professor Grimm. We'll run some promos of you standing in front of Harvard University, wearing a cap and gown. You'll explain to the viewers that your real name is Solomon Grimm and that you're a Harvard graduate. As Professor Grimm, you're going to take your opponents to school. Get it? You know, give them a lesson in wrestling. What do you think?"

Kronos heartily laughed off the suggestion. "But boss, I dint even finish da ninth grade," he told Mr. Collins. "I caint read no better den a toid grader. How'm I supposed ta be Professa Grimm? No tanks, I tink I'd radda wear da mask. Or how 'bout I just call myself Hoiman Boikowitz?"

At least that's how my father related the story to my mom and me, perfectly capturing Kronos' Bronx accent.

Mr. Collins still hasn't come up with another gimmick for Kronos. But he created a "rivalry" between Kronos and Black Mamba through a series of matches and interviews. This has led up to the Mask vs. Mask match that's set to take place at *The Final Stand*.

"Even after you're unmasked, we'll continue to call you Kronos until we can come up with something we can both agree on," Mr. Collins told him.

Sure, the bouts are *all* scripted. It's always decided ahead of time who's going to win each match. That's not a big secret anymore.

It bugs me, though, when people say that wrestling is fake and that wrestlers aren't real athletes.

Every time my father gets smacked with a metal folding chair, he really *does* get hit. Hard! When he gets thrown out of the ring and lands on the floor with a sickening thud, wrestling's critics dismiss it, saying, "But they know how to fall."

All wrestlers learn how to take bumps, that's a given. It's taught at every wrestling school. But no matter how well they may "know how to fall," that's still a concrete floor they're dropped on, with absolutely no give to it.

I sat at the lunch table trying to finish my plate of salmon patties—or at least what the cafeteria manager insisted were salmon patties—while a debate arose as to which wrestler was the toughest in the ACW.

"That's a no-brainer," said Terrance. "Bronko Savage, because he's the Iron Fist champion."

"Only until *The Final Stand*," said a curly-haired kid with glasses. "Jumbo Jefferson's gonna flatten him like a pancake with the Jumbo Splash."

"What about Butcher Murdock?" Goose asked, his mouth full of bread. "He's been the ACW champ three different times."

"Why don't you swallow your food before you talk?" Wendell scolded. "Murdock's never even beaten Ice Man Jacob Sloane."

"It doesn't matter, Wendy, 'cause he's beaten the Angel of Death twice," replied Goose.

"Quit calling me . . . " Suddenly Wendell became quiet. Everyone stared at Goose, then at me.

I smiled and shrugged to indicate that no offense had been taken.

Satisfied with my reaction, the guys rattled on with their discussion.

All around the cafeteria, groups of kids sat together, visiting, laughing, and talking about a zillion other things besides wrestling—movies, music, TV shows, books, video games. I wished I could leave my table and join them.

Then I spotted her. She was sitting near a window, spooning out a cup of yogurt, talking with a couple of other girls. What was her name? She sat in the third row in my English class. Samantha . . . Sandra . . . Sara . . . Sara! That's it. Sara with the straight, silky-smooth, light-brown hair, eyes as green as spring, and an inviting, dimpled smile that seemed to say, "Sure, Jesse, I'd love to spend some time with you."

Except that I hadn't gotten the nerve to even say "hi" to her yet.

She'd given a biographical oral presentation on the life of Edgar Allan Poe on my first day in that class. I was immediately blown away by her beauty and poise as she confidently shared her report.

A few days later, at the school library, I checked out a book of Edgar Allan Poe short stories. Up until then, the only one I was familiar with was "A Tell-Tale Heart." We'd read that one in my English class in St. Louis earlier in the year. But I wanted to be prepared to have something to talk about with Sara in case I ever mustered up the nerve to approach her. Besides, discussing "The Cask of Amontillado" or "The Pit and the Pendulum" would surely be more interesting to her than saying that my father was going to wrestle Prince Romulus at the next ACW pay-per-view event.

My daydream of Sara instantly vanished when I heard Goose mention Spirit's name.

"What did you say?" I asked.

"Hello? Anybody home?" Goose teased. He wiped his mouth with the back of his sleeve. "I've asked you twice already. What happened to Spirit? How come she's no longer your dad's valet?"

I could feel the early stages of a headache coming on. *Back! Just get back!* I mentally ordered it.

"I guess the ACW management decided they'd rather have her wrestle," I lied.

Terrance snorted. "She needs to go back to being a valet. She can't wrestle worth a dime."

"But you've gotta admit, guys," said Wendell with a goofy grin. "She is one hot babe."

"You got that right, Wendy. Aooohhh!" howled Goose.

"If I was *your* dad, I'd demand to have Spirit back as *my* valet," said Terrance. He hung his tongue out of his mouth and panted like a thirsty dog.

"Aooohhh!" Goose howled again.

We put away our trays and headed outside to the blacktop. Terrance ran and grabbed a basketball from the ball rack next to the gym.

We shot a few baskets before Wendell, all tired out, decided he'd rather stand against the wall and watch us play.

I didn't feel like playing much either, especially after the comments the guys made about Spirit.

The next time I got the ball, I took a shot at the hoop and missed. After that, I decided to call it quits and walked off the court.

Wendell's eyes lit up. I'm sure he thought I was going to join him. Instead, I headed in the opposite direction and turned the corner of the building. I wasn't in the mood to hear Wendell rant about his favorite subject. Maybe I could find something else to do to kill time until the bell rang.

Up ahead I saw Manny and Chester and Hugo huddled together behind the gym. I wondered what would be worse—turning around and having to listen to Wendell jabber about wrestling or risk getting taunted by Manny and his goons.

As I took a closer peek, I noticed they had someone surrounded against the wall. Someone who looked like . . . Sara?

"Let me go!" Sara screamed.

Hugo and Chester had her arms pinned back while Manny held her purse.

"Let's see what we got here," he said. He opened her bag and rifled through its contents. "Hey, six bucks." Manny stuffed the bills into his pocket. "Here's a hand-kerchief." He sniffed it, then tossed it to the ground. "A hairbrush . . . lipstick . . . "

"Leave her alone, you creeps!" yelled a girl with short black hair. I recognized her as one of the girls who had sat with Sara in the cafeteria.

Sara, now in tears, struggled to free herself, but Chester and Hugo held her tightly, hee-heeing like a pair of hyenas.

"Go get a teacher, Karen!" Sara told her friend.

Manny grabbed Karen by the wrist and pulled her toward him. "You're not going anywhere, *chula*."

After the horrible morning I'd had, the last thing I needed was to get involved in a confrontation with Manny and those other Neanderthals. But I had to help Sara, somehow.

I hesitated for a moment, then headed toward the wall.

"Leave them alone," I said. My voice cracked and the pitch came out higher than I had intended.

Manny whirled around and glared at me. "Take a hike, dork! You don't wanna mess with us."

He was right. I *didn't* want to mess with them. But it was too late. Trying to keep my voice from shaking I said, "D–Don't pick on the girls, that's all I'm saying." My throat dried up. Breathing became difficult. I could feel my heart slamming itself against the inside of my chest.

This time Manny released Karen's wrist. She ran off, hopefully to get some help. He stormed up to me. "Think you're tough enough to take me on, dork?" he asked.

"Look, Manny," I said. My right leg was now trembling out of control. "I–I don't want to fight you. I just want you to leave the girls alone."

Chester and Hugo let Sara loose. They stood alongside Manny with their arms crossed.

To my surprise, Sara remained where she was. I had expected her to run and join her friend Karen, but she didn't. Then I realized Manny still had Sara's purse in his hand and her money in his pocket.

"You wanna play hero, dork?" Manny growled. "The good guy? The knight in shining armor?" He punctuated his questions by gesturing quotation marks in the air with his fingers. "You're gonna wish you'd *never* gotten involved." He gave me a hard shove.

Chester and Hugo grinned and nodded, almost as if on cue.

Despite my fear, I managed to say, "Give her back her purse and money."

Manny sniggered. "You're something else, you know that? Well, c'mon, hero, you want it? Try to take it from me."

He took two steps back and dangled Sara's purse in front of me. With his other hand, he motioned me toward him.

"Get 'im, Manny!" cried his cheerleaders, Hugo and Chester.

A crowd quickly gathered. Manny circled around me, daring me to fight him. Some kids cried out, "Death! Death! Death! Death!"

"Give him the Death Drop Pile Driver!" shouted some moron from the crowd.

Oh, please, I thought, *give me a break.*

Nevertheless, that made Manny waver. He seemed a little unsure of himself. He glanced over at Chester and Hugo, to make sure they were there in case he needed them.

I had no intention of fighting Manny, unless I absolutely had to. And even if I did, there was no way I could apply my father's finishing maneuver on him. But Manny didn't know that. I could sense that he was wondering exactly what I was capable of.

The Death Drop Pile Driver appears devastating on TV. After my father weakens his opponents, he tosses them over his shoulder, turns them upside down, then he drives them, head first, onto the canvas, knocking them unconscious.

Except that it's all an illusion, like a magician's trick. No one ever gets hurt. Their heads never even touch the mat. But that's only because they practice it over and over. Otherwise, someone could get seriously injured.

Luckily for me, Manny didn't get a chance to find out if I could perform the Death Drop Pile Driver. Coach Johnson burst through the wall of kids that had fenced us in, followed by Karen and some other kids who had evidently heard about the confrontation.

"He's got my purse!" Sara shouted, stating the obvious. For the first time since confronting Manny, I realized how ridiculous he looked, standing there, holding a girl's purse in his hand. I had to smile.

Coach Johnson jerked the purse away from Manny. "You're going to the office, son."

"We were just horsing around, Coach, that's all," Manny said, feigning innocence.

"He also stole my money!" said Sara. "Six dollars. They're in his pocket."

From the expression on the coach's face, it didn't appear that he had any doubt that Sara was telling the truth. It seemed that Manny's reputation preceded him. "Let's have it," he ordered.

Realizing there was no point in denying it, Manny fished out the dollar bills from his pocket and slapped them in Coach Johnson's outstretched hand.

"Chester Leonard and Hugo Sanchez were part of it!" yelled Karen, scanning the crowd for them. But Manny's bookends had disappeared the moment the coach arrived.

"What about you?" Coach Johnson barked at me. "What's your story?"

"Jesse came to help us," Sara broke in before I could respond. "He made Manny and Chester and Hugo leave us alone."

I couldn't believe it. She knew my name. Sara knew who I was!

Coach Johnson grunted. Then he said to me, "You'd better come along, too, 'til we get everything straightened out."

"Yes, sir."

Manny glared at me as if to say, *This isn't over between us.*

I didn't care. I'd stood up to him. I had helped Sara. And she knew who I was. Things were finally starting to look up.

CHAPTER FOUR

"Jesse Baron?"

I poked my head out of my locker, glanced up, and smiled.

"Hi, I'm Sara Young." She extended a hand to me.

I rose from the floor with an armload of books. I tried to shake her hand, but my books began to spill.

"Oh, I'm sorry," she said. She helped me adjust them back into my arms. "Listen, I want to thank you for helping Karen and me out on the blacktop this morning." She flashed a wide, dimpled smile.

I shrugged modestly. "It was nothing. Glad I could help."

"I hope you didn't get in trouble with the principal for getting mixed up with Manny," she said.

"No, not at all. Coach Johnson explained what he saw to Dr. Seamster. Then I gave her my version of what happened. After that, I was sent back to class."

"You had just left the office when we walked in," said Sara. "Karen and I were called out of class, along with Chester and Hugo, to give our sides of the incident."

"Did Dr. Seamster do anything to them?"

Sara shook her head. "Nothing much. They got a three-day vacation from school. That's how much a suspension means to them."

"Well, at least the rest of the kids will have a three-day vacation from those bozos," I told her.

Sara smiled and nodded in agreement. "You're the wrestler's son, aren't you?"

"Yes, I am. Why? Are you a wrestling fan?"

She giggled. "No." Then she caught herself. "Please don't take offense, Jesse, but it's just that . . . well, my parents don't let me watch wrestling. They think it's . . . it's . . . "

"Junk, right?"

Sara blushed.

"That's okay." I said. "A lot of people feel that way about it. But it's how my father earns a living."

"Your parents bought the Bennetts' house," she said, changing the subject.

"How did you know?" I was surprised that this beautiful dream of a girl whom I had been gawking at for the past week seemed to know so much about me.

"My parents and the Bennetts have been friends for years. After they moved out of the neighborhood, the house sat vacant for about four months. Until your family bought it. We live a few houses down from yours."

An idea hit me. Before I could chicken out, I said, "Would you like to walk home with me, Sara? I–I mean, if you're not hanging out with your friends or anything."

To my delight, she said, "Sure. Just let me run and tell Karen I won't be going home with her."

While she spoke to her friend, I gathered my books and stuffed them into my backpack.

When she was ready, Sara and I squeezed out the front door through the piles of students that were congregated there and headed up the sidewalk.

"Death! Death! Death! Death!" some kids shouted out the windows from the school buses parked along the curb as we passed by.

Sara turned to me with a worried look on her face.

I laughed. "Ignore them. It's not as creepy as it sounds. That's what they chant for my father."

By the baffled look on her face, I knew Sara had no idea what I was talking about. But then, not being a wrestling fan, I didn't expect her to understand.

We crossed the street, turned the corner, and headed for the quarter mile walk home.

"That took a lot of courage, standing up to Manny and Chester and Hugo the way you did out on the blacktop," said Sara. "Weren't you scared they might hurt you?"

I shrugged. "Not really. I figured help was coming. Anyway, *you* were the one they were hurting. I couldn't just look the other way and pretend I hadn't seen anything. I had to stop them."

"But, Jesse, what if they beat you up or something? They're the biggest bullies in school."

It felt nice to hear her sound so concerned about me.

"Sara, do you know what frightens kids the most about fighting?" I asked. "They're afraid of the pain from getting hit."

"Well, of course they are," she said. "Are you going to tell me you're not afraid of pain?"

"No, not exactly. But I once asked my father how he could handle getting punched and stomped and gouged and slapped all the time. He told me, 'We're in the hurting business, Jesse. It's part of the job. But once you come to terms with the fact that no matter what, you're going to get hit at some point, you learn to expect and accept the pain. After that, it doesn't hurt nearly as much.'"

"The 'hurting business,'" Sara said. "That's an interesting way of putting what your father does for a living. I guess then, in a way, my dad is in the 'protection business.'"

"Why? Is he in the Mafia or something?" I teased.

"No, he's a police officer."

"Really? My father wanted to be a cop for a while."

"A cop?" Sara laughed. "How would he arrest criminals? By giving them the Death Drop Pile Driver?"

That made me chuckle. "I thought you said you didn't watch wrestling."

"I don't," she replied. "I don't even know what a Death Drop Pile Driver is. It's just something I hear kids say whenever they talk about your dad."

"Well, my father wasn't born the Angel of Death, you know," I told her. "Long before that, he was Mark Baron, criminal justice major at the University of Texas in Austin. He planned to join the San Antonio Police Department after graduation."

Sara frowned. With a tinge of disdain in her voice, she said, "I suppose he found being the Angel of Death more thrilling than fighting crime."

"No, that's not it," I told her. "He didn't become the Angel of Death until years later. He used to play football in college, defensive tackle. His teammates nicknamed him the 'Mangler' because of the brutal way he sacked opposing quarterbacks. Anyway, in his senior year, he was drafted by the Dallas Cowboys."

"Your dad played for the Dallas Cowboys?" Sara asked in astonishment. This obviously impressed her much more than knowing that my father was the Angel of Death.

"No, he never had a chance to play for them. During training camp, he tore some tendons on his right knee and had to have surgery. While he was recuperating, the Cowboys cut him."

Sara seemed momentarily distracted. Something down the street had grabbed her attention. "Hey, there's a *paletero*." She pointed at an old man pushing a green cart.

"A what?" I asked.

"He's an ice cream vendor. Don't tell me you've never bought an ice cream from a *paletero*?"

"I'm such a deprived child," I said, faking a sad face.

"Come on," said Sara. "It's my treat, my reward to you for rescuing me this morning."

We crossed the street and approached the *paletero*. He was a hunched-back, old Mexican man. He wore a weather-beaten brown hat that matched his weather-beaten brown face. On his cart, various pictures were pasted of the kinds of frozen treats he sold. The push handle of his wagon had a small bicycle bell attached to it, which he rang as he walked to attract customers.

"I want you to try the watermelon-flavored ice cream," said Sara. "It's my favorite." She turned to the vendor. "*Dos de sandía, por favor.*"

I stared at her, amazed. "You spoke to him in Spanish!"

"Well, I would have asked him in Chinese, but I'm a little rusty at it," Sara said, jokingly. "Of course I spoke to him in Spanish, silly." She took the ice creams and her change from the *paletero*. "*Gracias.*"

The old man smiled appreciatively. He headed down the street, pushing his cart, ringing his bicycle bell. Soon he was surrounded by a group of little kids, anxious to sample the *paletero*'s treats.

"My mom's Mexican," Sara explained. "She was born in Monterrey. Her family moved to the United States when she was a little girl. How about you, Jesse? *¿Hablas español?*"

"*Muy poquito*," I replied. "My parents are much more fluent in Spanish than I am, but we mostly just speak English at home."

"*Qué lástima*," Sara said with a sigh.

We stopped under a tree and ate our ice creams. I could see why Sara's favorite flavor was watermelon. It was delicious.

"I didn't mean to interrupt your story about your dad," said Sara. "What happened to him after he got cut from the Dallas Cowboys?"

"Well, at that point, he had pretty much decided to become a police officer," I continued. "He was going to move back here, to San Antonio. But while he was working out in a gym in Dallas, a man named Luke Winston approached him. He was an ex-professional wrestler. Luke Winston suggested that my father try his hand at wrestling. He told him that he still had some contacts in the business if he was interested."

"Is that how he became the Angel of Death?" Sara asked.

Having gobbled up my "reward," I looked down the street for the *paletero*. My taste buds hungered for another watermelon-flavored ice cream, but the old man was gone.

"That's how he broke into the wrestling profession," I said, "but he was still a few years away from being the Angel of Death. His first ring name was The Mangler, his college nickname. Actually, he was called Mark 'The Mangler' Baron. He played a 'face.'"

"What do you mean, he played a *face*?" Sara wanted to know.

"In wrestling, Sara, a 'baby face' or a 'face' is a 'good guy.' The 'bad guys' are called 'heels,'" I explained. "My father wore burnt-orange tights and white boots, the colors of his alma mater, the University of Texas. The number 78, his old football jersey number, was stitched to the back of his trunks. His boots sported pictures of Texas longhorns, the school's mascot. Fans used to show up in droves to watch him wrestle, mainly because they remembered him from his football days at UT."

"So when did he become the Angel of Death?" Sara seemed to be growing impatient. For someone who didn't watch wrestling, she sure seemed to take a lot of interest in my father's career.

"Do you know what my father looks like?" I asked.

She shook her head. "I told you, I'm not allowed to watch wrestling."

"Well, my father's six feet, seven inches tall. He weighs around 320 pounds. With his size, it was difficult to continue promoting him as a face. So after his stint as The Mangler, he wore a black and silver mask and played a heel called the Annihilator. He wrestled as the Annihilator for a good part of his career until he signed up with American Championship Wrestling."

"That's when he became the Angel of Death, right?" said Sara.

"Yes. Frank Collins, the ACW promoter, likes to create his own characters. He usually doesn't allow wrestlers to keep the gimmicks they've used with another organization unless it's a character that's real popular with the fans."

"And I take it that as the Annihilator, your dad wasn't a well-known wrestler," said Sara.

"He was mostly known in the Southwest. My father's early career was spent in the independent circuit. He wrestled for small organizations in and around Texas. When he hired on with the ACW, Mr. Collins created the Angel of Death persona. My father grew his hair out long, past his shoulders, and dyed it a darker shade of black than it already was. A makeup artist with the company developed the design for his skeleton face."

"A skeleton face?" Sara asked, bemused.

I nodded. "It generally takes about an hour to apply the makeup. But the effect is awesome. My father also wears black leather tights, a sleeveless black leather shirt, and black boots. He enters the ring draped in a black robe and carrying a scythe."

"He sounds fantastic!" exclaimed Sara. "How long has he been the Angel of Death?"

"For about five years," I told her.

"I'd love to see him," she said. "If only my parents would let me watch the show."

"Hey, no problem. I've got millions of photos of him. My house is up ahead. If you want to come in, I'll . . . "

My voice trailed off as I remembered the scene with my mom at breakfast. I had no idea what sort of mood she'd be in.

"Um, we'd better make it another time," I said awkwardly. "I've got a ton of homework to do, and I need to get on it right away."

"Sure, Jesse, I understand," said Sara, but by the tone in her voice, I wasn't so sure she did.

I was stupid to invite her over, then cut her off like that.

A couple of minutes later, we arrived at my house.

"I'll see you at school tomorrow, okay?" said Sara.

"Yeah, okay. And thanks for the ice cream."

I opened the door and braced myself for whatever might happen inside.

CHAPTER FIVE

"Mom?" I called uneasily.

"I'm over here in the dining room."

I dropped my backpack in the foyer and followed the sound of her voice.

The dining room was cluttered with stacks of cardboard boxes. They'd been sitting there ever since we moved to our house, and up until now, my mom hadn't gotten around to unpacking them. What few meals we ate at home, we ate at the breakfast table in the kitchen.

She was wearing a pair of faded jeans and a St. Louis Rams T-shirt. From one of the boxes, she was removing some dishes and arranging them in the china cabinet.

"Hi." I made my way through the maze of boxes and kissed her cheek.

"How was school?"

She routinely asked me that, with my expected response being "fine." But I could sense a harshness in her voice. It didn't have the usual warm tone. Perhaps she was still mad about the morning.

"Fine," I said.

"Really?" There was a definite coldness. "Did anything unusual happen at school today?"

"Just the regular stuff. I met a girl, Sara Young. She and her family live nearby. They're friends of the Bennetts — you know, the people we bought the house from."

"Jesse, sit down," my mother said, ignoring what I was telling her.

She cleared two large boxes of framed photos from the table. I sat down across from her.

"First of all, I want to tell you how sorry I am for what happened this morning," she began. "I was upset that Dad's plans were changed at the last minute and he couldn't come home today, so I took my frustration out on you. I shouldn't have done that."

"That's okay, Mom," I told her. "It was my fault, too. I spilled my juice on you, and I should've been more careful."

She shut her eyes and lowered her head, as if she was praying. Maybe she was. Finally she gazed deeply at me. "Jesse, you know things have been pretty strained between Dad and me lately."

Suddenly my stomach tightened into a knot. *Oh, no,* I thought. *Please don't tell me you're going to leave him again.*

"I've tried very hard to make things work for us. And I honestly believe things are going to get better. But, Jesse . . . " Her voice grew louder. "We *all* have to pull together, do you understand?"

"Sure, Mom," I said.

"Things are tense enough around here without *you* adding to the problems."

What did she mean by that? I was confused.

"Mom, I said I was sorry about the juice. I don't know what else to tell you. If you're talking about your dress—"

"I'm talking about your school, Jesse!" She slammed her hand on the table.

"My school?"

"I got a call a little while ago from your homeroom teacher, Mrs. Petrosky. She told me that you failed your history test today, that you received the lowest grade in the class."

Now it was my turn to get angry. "There was no way I could have passed that test, Mom, and she knew it! It was on the Texas Revolution. I know you and Dad grew up here in Texas, but *I* didn't. It was impossible for me to learn all that stuff in a week and a half, when the rest of the class has been studying it forever."

"Your teacher didn't seem to think so, Jesse. She told me she gave you plenty of time to prepare for it."

"But, Mom," I argued, "the test covered six chapters! Look, I'll get my book and show you if you don't believe me." I started to rise from the table.

"Sit down, Jesse!" she ordered. "That's not all. Mrs. Petrosky also told me you got into a fight today at lunchtime."

"What? I didn't get in a fight!"

My mom's eyes widened. "Are you going to tell me that your teacher called and made all this up? Are you calling your teacher a liar?"

"No, Mom, but—"

"Jesse, please!"

A flash of pain shot through my head like a charge of electricity.

Back when I could still talk to my mom about my headaches, she diagnosed them as being "stress-induced." I've never seen a doctor about them, but if I did, I'm sure he would agree with her.

"Mrs. Petrosky wants to come by tomorrow afternoon to discuss the problems you're having at school."

"But I'm not *having* any problems at school," I insisted.

She grabbed a tissue from a box on top of the buffet table and wiped her eyes. We don't ordinarily keep a tissue box in the dining room, which made me wonder how much crying she'd done all day.

"Well, your teacher seems to think you do." The tension in her voice had begun to fade. "I suggested having a conference with her at school, but she kindly offered to come here. Mrs. Petrosky wants to share some ideas that might help you bring up your grade. She seems to be a very caring teacher, Jesse. Please don't give her any trouble."

"But I don't."

The pounding in my head grew stronger. There was no point in arguing with her. She had made up her mind about what I was going through at school, and nothing I could say was going to make her think otherwise.

"I need to get started on my homework," I said.

As I rose from the table, I spotted a box of photo albums on the floor. I thought I'd pick out a few pictures to show Sara tomorrow. "Is it all right if I take this to my room?"

"Be my guest. I need to get all this mess put away before your teacher's visit. I don't want her to get the impression that we're a bunch of slobs."

I grabbed the box and retreated to my room.

It had been a long time since I'd gone through our photo albums. I fished out a couple of them and stretched across my bed on my stomach. My headache eased a little, but still remained, keeping a steady, metronome-like beat.

The first album I flipped through had pictures of my father in his Mangler days. There was one of him shaking hands with Ox Mulligan, a wrestler my father used to watch when he was little. There was another one of my father holding the Texas Heavyweight belt. It was his first championship title.

After flipping through a few more pages, I closed the book and tossed it back in the box. I opened a blue and gold album. This one had more recent photographs. On the first page was an 8x10 glossy of my father in his Angel of Death outfit, surrounded by flames. The words, ANGEL OF DEATH, were formed with black, smoky letters. It was the same picture often found on lunch boxes, backpacks, and T-shirts. I would definitely share this one with Sara. I slipped it out of its clear plastic cover and set it on top of my nightstand.

The next two pages had pictures of him wrestling Jumbo Jefferson. In a couple of them, Jefferson's face was masked with blood. Too gory, I decided. Sara wouldn't understand.

When I turned the page, I was stunned by what I saw. There was a photo of my father, as the Angel of Death, posed with a blank space. The blank space should've been his former valet, Spirit, but her picture had been ripped out. I flipped through the other pages. Every image of Spirit was missing, torn off each photograph.

My mom had done it, of course.

She'd never been comfortable with Spirit being teamed with my father. The pairing had been Frank Collins' idea.

When my father first signed on with the American Championship Wrestling organization, he wrestled as a "mid-carder" — a wrestler who hasn't yet been elevated to main event status. He wrestled "jobbers" like Wally Armstrong and Johnny Surfer. Jobbers are wrestlers who "lose" every match. Their job is to help push mid-carders to become top-tier wrestlers. That is, if the promoters feel that the mid-carders have the potential to headline a show. My father did.

Once he became a featured star, Mr. Collins decided that my father needed a valet, someone to escort him to the ring, to hold his robe and scythe during his match.

A woman named Cassandra Richardson had just begun to work for the ACW. She primarily wrestled "house shows," so she wasn't familiar to most fans. House shows are wrestling events that aren't shown on television. Only the Monday night shows are televised. She wasn't a very good wrestler, and Mr. Collins knew it.

But rather than letting her go, he created the character of Spirit and paired her up with my father.

Spirit has long, wavy, red hair. She wears a white, shiny, skintight, leather jumpsuit with light-blue high-heeled boots and gloves. Her character is a sharp contrast to my father's dark, brooding, sinister-looking presence. Everyone instantly fell in love with Spirit.

Everyone, except my mom.

At first she didn't say much. But as the popularity of the Angel of Death and Spirit continued to grow, the ACW increased their number of public appearances, both at TV tapings and at house shows.

"You spend more time with that woman than you do with me," my mom would often complain to my father.

"It's just business, Molly, you know that," he tried to assure her. "The gimmick is working well for the company."

"Well, it's not working well for us!"

This was one of the reasons she left him.

Before my parents got back together again, my mom demanded that my father get rid of Spirit as his valet.

After discussing the situation with his boss, Mr. Collins reluctantly agreed to separate them.

The Angel of Death now enters the ring alone. An ACW staff member meets him inside the ring. My father hands him the accessories to his costume, and the worker carries them back to the dressing room once the match begins.

As for Spirit, she returned to wrestling. But Terrance was right. She can't wrestle worth a dime.

While I dug in the box for another album, I came across a plastic action figure of the Angel of Death. It was one of the first models the ACW put on the market. There have been six different Angel of Death toys in all, but I don't think any of them look like him.

I stood the action figure on my bed's headboard shelf, then drew another album from the box. This one didn't contain any wrestling photographs. They were only family pictures. My mom insists on keeping the photos separate.

There was one of me sitting naked in the bathtub. I must've been about two years old. Still, there was no way Sara would ever see this one.

I turned a few pages. There were pictures of my mom, Aunt Gracie, and me at Disney World. My father was supposed to go with us, but the ACW had him wrestle a number of matches that week, so Aunt Gracie took his place.

The next page had pictures of me in the dinosaur program our second grade class performed when we lived in Atlanta. Or was it Memphis? My mom had sewn my stegosaurus costume. I remember thinking that the bony plates on the back looked more like tiny wings. I also remember that my father didn't see the show.

He also missed my performance in "Jack and the Beanstalk" when I was in the fourth grade. I had a tiny part, just one of the town folks in the background that Jack passed as he went to sell his cow. We had just moved to Charlotte, North Carolina. The kids were practicing for the program when I was enrolled in the class. My teacher, Mrs. Harrison, didn't want to exclude me from the production, so she stuck me in the crowd scene where kids who couldn't act were placed.

Last year we moved to St. Louis. There, I joined the school band. The band director assigned me to play the drums. I told him I wanted to learn to play the trumpet, but he said that I would better serve the band by being in the percussion section. I think he must have seen my school records and figured I wouldn't last long in that school, anyway. He probably didn't want to invest the time to teach me how to play the trumpet since I'd probably be gone before the school year was out. We had two band concerts. My father didn't attend either one.

I closed the album and dumped it in with the others. I picked up the 8x10 photo I'd set aside for Sara and studied it.

What was it Wendell had said to me? "You must be the luckiest kid in the world to have the Angel of Death for a father."

Somehow, I didn't feel all that lucky.

CHAPTER SIX

"Psst!"

It was my third try but I still couldn't get Adela Crager's attention. She had her nose deeply buried in her book.

My English teacher, Mr. Gillette, begins his class with silent reading time. For the first fifteen minutes of the period, all students are required to read quietly from a book of their choice.

Adela must be reading a great story, I thought, although I didn't recall her being much of a reader.

"Psst! Adela!" I shouted in a loud whisper. Adela's head jerked up. She glanced around the room, startled, her eyelids at half-mast.

I should've known Adela was asleep. I'd heard her read aloud. Adela Crager was no reader.

"Psst!" I said again.

She turned and stared at me, her eyelids fluttering.

"Pass this down to Sara," I whispered, handing her a green pocket folder.

Adela glared at me, irritated that I'd woken her up. Looking down at the folder, she grudgingly snatched it from my hand and tossed it onto Sara's desk.

Sara turned away from her book, *Something Wicked This Way Comes*. She stared at the folder. She glanced over, first at Adela, then at me. I grinned, pointed at my chest, then at the folder to indicate that it had come from me. Sara smiled and nodded.

Adela reopened her book and went back to sleep.

I watched for Sara's reaction as she drew out the 8 x 10 glossy from the folder. Her jaw dropped, and her eyes widened in surprise. She turned to me and mouthed the words "He's incredible!"

I smiled. For the first time in quite a while I was proud to let someone know that the Angel of Death was my father. Since she didn't watch wrestling, I had worried about what Sara would think when she saw the photo. I was glad she liked it.

While Sara studied the picture and I studied Sara, neither one of us noticed Mr. Gillette approaching her desk. Suddenly his hand reached down and snatched the photograph away from her.

He stared at the picture and wrinkled his nose as if he'd just detected a foul odor.

"Quite frankly, Miss Young, I find it disappointing that you would take an interest in this type of vulgar entertainment." He folded the photograph in half and stuffed it into his blazer pocket. "Now, I would appreciate it if you would be so kind as to spend the rest of the allotted silent reading time doing what you are supposed to be doing—*reading!*"

So strongly did he emphasize the word "reading" that it nearly jolted Adela Crager out of her seat. Her book flew out of her hands and fell on the floor. Dazed, Adela searched around her desk, trying to spot where her book had landed.

Mr. Gillette scowled at me. "Mr. Baron, your father's celebrity status does not impress me, whatsoever. If you want to peddle these tasteless, disgusting photographs, I suggest you do it on your own time. Not mine!"

He wheeled around and headed back to his desk.

I looked at Sara and shrugged.

She smiled and returned the shrug.

How could I have been so dumb? I knew I should've waited until lunchtime to give her the picture. The last thing I wanted was to see Sara get in trouble, especially on my account.

I looked up at Mr. Gillette. He had perched himself on his desk, his arms folded across his chest, and was eyeing us like a hawk. I figured he'd probably hand the photograph over to my homeroom teacher, which would give Mrs. Petrosky something else to discuss with my mom about all the "problems" I was having in school.

Interestingly, during history class earlier in the day, Mrs. Petrosky didn't mention a word to me about her upcoming visit to my house or about my failing grade. She simply went about her business, talking about the Battle of San Jacinto and of Mexican President Santa Anna's eventual capture.

The only time she spoke to me was while the class was copying down notes from the chalkboard. She strolled up to my desk and asked, "Will your father be home this evening?"

When I told her he wouldn't, she looked disappointed. Then she composed herself and continued teaching.

As soon as my English class had ended, I caught up with Sara in the hallway.

"Sara, listen, I'm sorry I got you in trouble with Mr. Gillette. I shouldn't have given you the picture until after class."

"That's okay, Jesse. Your dad's absolutely amazing! He looks like a comic book superhero."

"Too bad Mr. Gillette took away your picture. Come on, let's see if he'll give it back."

When we reentered his classroom, Mr. Gillette was straightening the desks, preparing his room for the next group of students. He was muttering something that was mostly inaudible, but included, " . . . a bunch of bone-heads."

"Mr. Gillette?"

He turned around, startled.

"May I please have the picture I gave to Sara?" I asked.

My teacher glared at me. "Mr. Baron, in case you haven't figured it out by now, I happen to take a great deal of pride in my classroom. I expect each one of my students to put forth his or her best effort—including you! I am also aware of what your father does for a living, and to be quite honest, I find it to be an unseemly profession. But that's just my opinion. In any case, I will not tolerate you disrupting my class by distributing this garbage while you should be reading."

He fished out the photograph from his coat pocket and scrutinized it.

"Imagine," he said with a look of contempt, "grown men parading around in their underpants, grunting and growling, pretending to beat each other. If there is any lower form of entertainment—"

"May I have it back, sir?" Sara asked gently. "Please?"

Mr. Gillette frowned. "Certainly not!"

With that, he ripped the photograph in two. Then he tore the pieces once more.

Sara gasped in disbelief.

"Now go on to your next class!" Mr. Gillette shooed us away with the back of his hand.

I couldn't believe what he'd done. How could he be so thoughtless, so cruel? My heart pulsated with rage. Without thinking, I shouted, "You had no right to tear that picture! I gave it to Sara."

"Mr. Baron! This is *my* classroom and I make the rules here, not you," he growled, shoving his index finger in my face. "And I will do whatever I want. Next time, you will think twice about bringing that schlock in here."

Thump-thump! Thump-thump! Thump-thump! Thump-thump!

"Get out of here, both of you. Unless you wish to add insolence to your misconduct."

I remained standing there for a few seconds, desperately fighting back the tears that I could feel surfacing. The last thing I needed was for Sara to see me cry.

"I'll get you another one," I told her.

She stared at the shreds of paper in our teacher's hand. "You didn't have to do that," she said under her breath.

Ignoring her, Mr. Gillette tossed the scraps into the trash can and continued straightening his desks.

Out in the hallway, Sara broke down crying. "I despise that man!"

"It's okay, don't worry about it," I said. "Besides, it was my fault. I shouldn't have taken that picture out in the first place."

"He thinks he's such a great teacher," sniffed Sara. "Well, he may know a lot about literature, but he doesn't know a thing about working with kids." She shuddered and wiped away her tears with her hand.

It pained me to see her so upset. Her crying also magnified my growing headache.

"I'd like you to meet my father sometime," I said. "He's not home right now, but I'll try to work something out, okay?"

"Sure." Sara smiled. "I'd like that."

"We'd better hurry to class. We don't want to be late."

"Okay." She wiped her eyes again. "I'll see you at lunch."

CHAPTER SEVEN

At around five thirty in the evening, I heard a car pull into the driveway. I peeked out my window and spotted Mrs. Petrosky getting out of a silver Honda.

I slipped my homework in my math book. I figured I wouldn't get back to it until after she left. I'm sure my mom expected me to sit in on the conference.

Even though I knew Mrs. Petrosky had arrived, I decided to wait until she rang the doorbell before I met her. I didn't want to appear anxious or nervous about her visit. *I'll let my mom welcome her in.*

It seemed strange having a teacher come to our house, especially one I hardly knew. Even stranger to me was what she thought was so all-fired important that she felt the need to make the trip here. Why didn't she talk to my mom during regular school hours? After all, my mom had offered to meet with her in the classroom.

I'd find out soon enough.

The doorbell rang. I heard my mom greet her.

A moment later, there was a knock at my door. My mom poked her head inside my room. "Jesse, your teacher's here."

When we entered the den, Mrs. Petrosky was snapping pictures like crazy from a disposable camera.

"Please forgive me," she said, slightly embarrassed. "It's just that I've never been inside a real celebrity's home. I hope you don't mind."

"No, of course not," my mom replied, but I knew better. She's always been uncomfortable around camera bugs and autograph hounds who constantly pester my father whenever we go out in public as a family.

Mrs. Petrosky snapped another picture, one of a replica of my father's ACW heavyweight title belt, which hung above the fireplace mantle, before she acknowledged my presence.

"Hello, Jesse. It's good to see you," she said warmly, even though I'd spent my first and last class periods in her room.

"Please sit down," my mom said.

Mrs. Petrosky remained standing, gazing at the photographs hanging on the walls. She took a picture of a photograph of my father posing with Jason Cage and Sean LaRue, the Midnight Raiders.

"Mrs. Petrosky?" my mom called.

"Oh, I'm sorry. I guess I got a little carried away. You have such a fascinating place, Mrs. Baron," she said, gazing around the room. "By any chance, will your husband be home any time soon?"

I'd already told her at school that he wouldn't be home until Friday.

"No, I'm afraid he's out of town . . . working."

Mrs. Petrosky giggled. "Yes, of course. Working." She slipped the camera inside a large tote bag.

She sat next to my mom on our green leather couch. I sat across from them on the matching love seat.

"Mrs. Baron, I want you to know that I'm one of your husband's biggest fans. I never miss *Monday Night Mayhem*. As a matter of fact, back in February, a friend of mine and I had a chance to see him wrestle the Black Mamba live at the Alamodome when the ACW came to town. Your husband won the match, of course." She flashed my mom a wide, toothy grin.

"Thank you, Mrs. Petrosky. Now, about Jesse . . . "

"Do you suppose it would be possible for me to get your husband's autograph? I brought my autograph book with me." She took out a small book from her tote bag. "I know he's not home at the moment, but maybe if I left it here, he could sign it when he gets in. Then Jesse can return it to me at school."

My mom forced herself to smile. "Yes, I guess that can be arranged. Now, about Jesse . . . "

"I also brought a picture that I'd like your husband to autograph, if that's all right."

Mrs. Petrosky pulled out an Angel of Death 8x10 glossy from her tote bag. It was a copy of the one I'd given Sara that Mr. Gillette ripped up. They sell them at all ACW events. I wondered what Mr. Gillette would think if he knew that Mrs. Petrosky had the same photograph. Would he rip it up, too?

My mom placed the photograph and the autograph book on the coffee table.

"Mrs. Petrosky, on the phone, you told me that you had some suggestions on how to help Jesse be more successful in school," she said with growing exasperation.

My teacher didn't respond. Her eyes were deeply fixated on the walls.

"Mrs. Petrosky?"

"Hmm?"

"You told me that Jesse hadn't done well on his history test, that he had received the lowest score in the class."

"Oh . . . yes," my teacher replied, finally waking up from her trance. "Well, to be perfectly honest with you, Mrs. Baron, Jesse's wasn't the lowest grade. Actually, there were a few others who scored lower. But those students are, for the most part, troublemakers who don't care about their grades. Three of them are currently on suspension for trying to mug a couple of girls out on the blacktop."

The "three of them," of course, were the Three Stooges—Manny, Chester, and Hugo.

"Luckily, Jesse stopped those boys from hurting the girls," my teacher added. She patted me on the knee and smiled.

"Is that how Jesse got involved in a fight?" my mom asked.

"I *wasn't* in a fight," I protested.

Mrs. Petrosky chuckled nervously. "Jesse didn't exactly get in a fight, Mrs. Baron. From what Coach Johnson told me, Jesse merely ordered those boys to leave the girls alone."

My mom had a confused look on her face. It was pretty clear that the version of the events my teacher had related on the phone was different from what she was now saying.

"Is Jesse having difficulty adjusting to his new school?" My mom probed for new information since there seemed to be a discrepancy between their initial conversation and this one. "Because we *have* moved quite a bit, due to my husband's job. Unfortunately, Jesse's been in so many schools over the years that by the time he gets used to one place, we have to move again. But we're planning to make San Antonio our permanent home. My husband and I both grew up here and . . . and . . . Mrs. Petrosky?"

My teacher's eyes had begun to rove again, and my mom knew she wasn't paying attention to her.

"What do you want us to do, Mrs. Petrosky?" she asked loudly.

"Hmm? About what?"

With frustration in her voice, my mom cried, "About Jesse! Didn't you tell me on the phone that he was doing poorly in your history class? That he had failed your test on the Texas Revolution?"

Mrs. Petrosky said, "Well, that's understandable, Mrs. Baron, given that Jesse has been in my class for such a short time."

"I told you, Mom," I said.

Ignoring me, my mom continued. "Is there anything Jesse can do to make up his failing grade? After I got off the phone with you, I thought it might be a good idea to take Jesse to visit the Alamo and some of the other Spanish missions in the city. I remember visiting those places many times when I was a child. As a matter of fact, my parents even bought me a Davy Crockett 'coonskin cap that I wore all the time." She smiled sheepishly.

By the glassy look in her eyes, I could tell that Mrs. Petrosky had begun to drift off again. She was barely listening to what my mom was saying.

At last she reentered the conversation. "I'd like to offer a suggestion that could erase the 'F' Jesse received on his test."

"Of course," said my mom eagerly.

I sat up, all ears. I figured she was going to ask me to write a report about the Alamo or about some Texas hero. After I failed a major science test when we lived in Omaha, my teacher had me write a research paper on the life of Thomas Edison to make up my low grade.

Mrs. Petrosky paused and collected her thoughts. She cleared her throat. "My class falls under the umbrella of social studies, Mrs. Baron. And as I'm sure you're aware, social studies branches out into many different areas besides history—for instance, the community, let's say." She reached across the coffee table and picked up the 8x10 glossy photo of my father. "If the Angel of Death and perhaps some of the other ACW wrestlers were to make an appearance at Lanier Middle School—we could call it 'career investigations'—then Jesse's 'F' could easily be replaced by an 'A.'" She grinned like the proverbial cat that had just swallowed the canary.

If my mom didn't see through her, I sure did. Suddenly it became crystal clear what her plan was and why she had come here. It was all a setup. She wasn't concerned about my doing poorly on that history test. She hadn't called my mom to discuss my "problems" at school. It was a ruse to meet my father—to see where her favorite wrestler, the Angel of Death, lived.

"I–I'm not quite sure it can be arranged," said my mom, flustered. "You see, all public appearances by ACW wrestlers must be approved by the organization's management. You would have to contact their offices."

Mrs. Petrosky frowned. Not about to be swayed, she said, "Surely there are exceptions . . . under *special circumstances*. An 'F' is not easy to make up, especially when Jesse has enrolled so late in the year. I'm simply offering an alternate solution, Mrs. Baron."

I couldn't believe what I was hearing. This was blackmail, pure and simple.

Produce the Angel of Death, lady, or the kid fails the class.

"I can write a report on Davy Crockett or William Travis or any other Texas hero, if that will help," I offered.

My mom looked at my teacher hopefully.

But Mrs. Petrosky pretended not to hear me. She rose from the couch, indicating that the conference was over. "Talk it over with your husband, Mrs. Baron. I'm sure we can come to some sort of agreement."

My mom stood and walked her to the foyer. "I will, but please try to understand, I can't make any promises."

Mrs. Petrosky gave her a used car salesman smile. "I only have Jesse's best interest at heart. You understand that, don't you, Mrs. Baron? I just want him to succeed."

My mom nodded weakly.

Mrs. Petrosky reached her hand into her tote bag and grabbed her camera. "Do you mind if I take your picture?"

Before my mom could reply, Mrs. Petrosky snapped two quick shots. "Thank you, Mrs. Baron. It was a pleasure to meet you. You have a lovely home." She opened the door and let herself out. "I'll see you at school tomorrow, Jesse," she said with a wiggle of her fingers.

In St. Louis, my friend Eric and I once attended a carnival that was set up on the parking lot of an old shopping center. There was a man running a game where he slipped a ball into one of three cups. Then he shuffled the cups around, and for a dollar, you could guess in which cup the ball was. If you guessed correctly, you'd win a stuffed Tweety Bird or Sylvester doll. Together, Eric and I must've spent over fifteen dollars trying to guess which cup had the ball. Neither one of us won. Even as we walked away, dejected and broke, the man kept challenging us to try it one more time.

Watching Mrs. Petrosky getting into her car, I had the sinking feeling that, once again, I was being conned.

CHAPTER EIGHT

"Dad!"

I rushed through the airline terminal to meet him. He arrived with another wrestler—a man named Carlos Montoya. Wrestling fans never recognize Carlos Montoya in public, though. He wrestles under a mask and is better known as El Azteca Dorado—The Golden Aztec. For that matter, without the skeleton face paint and his wrestling attire, fans don't immediately recognize my father, either.

"How are you, champ?" he said, handing me his duffel bag. "Where's Mom?"

"Over there."

I pointed to a row of chairs. My mom had remained seated even after my father's plane landed.

"What happened to your head?" I asked.

He had a huge gauze bandage on his forehead, held down with two strips of tape.

"Oh . . . Butcher Murdock," my father replied with a shrug, as if that was all the explanation needed. And indeed, it was.

I've seen my father fight Don "Butcher" Murdock bunches of times. Their matches sometimes involve Murdock smashing him over the head with a metal folding chair.

My father's forehead generally opens up and streams of blood flow out. The bleeding, though, is seldom the result of the chair shots.

Wrestlers use a technique called "blading" or "juicing" to achieve that effect. Earlier in the day, before they wrestle, they swallow several aspirins. This helps thin the blood in their systems. Then, just prior to their match, they hide a small razor blade, usually in their wristbands or in their tights. At a strategic point during the bout, when a wrestler is struck with a "foreign object," he slips the blade out and scrapes his forehead with it, slicing into tiny vessels. The combination of the thinned blood, the perspiration, and the physical energy of the match itself causes the blood to gush out. According to my father, it stings like crazy, but it's not nearly as painful or as devastating as it may appear to the audience. Frank Collins calls on certain performers to blade from time to time in order to add realism to their matches. Unfortunately, my father's forehead is permanently disfigured with thick, ugly scars from countless blading jobs. I wouldn't want to go through life looking like that.

We walked over to my mom.

"Hello, Molly," my father greeted her.

She sighed, then with some reluctance, rose to her feet.

"Hi," she said without emotion. Gently, she ran her fingers across his bandage, but didn't say anything about it. Long ago, she accepted those kinds of injuries as part of the job. Finally she reached up and kissed him lightly. "Glad you're home."

He pulled away and turned to his friend. "You know Carlos, don't you?

"*Buenas tardes, señora.*" Carlos Montoya took her hand and kissed it. "*Gusto de verla otra vez.*"

"*Igualmente,* Carlos," my mom replied with the first smile I'd seen on her all day.

We headed toward the baggage claim area in uneasy silence. Even Carlos could sense that there was tension between my parents. Or perhaps my father had confided in him — discussed his home situation. They've been friends ever since Carlos joined the company about a year ago. We stood quietly, watching suitcases and bags clumsily ride the carousel.

"There's ours," I said, breaking the silence. I reached over and grabbed my father's luggage — two large suitcases and a garment bag.

We remained standing there a few moments longer and waited for Carlos to retrieve his bags.

"Let's go eat somewhere," said my father. "I'm starving."

My mom groaned. "It's past midnight, Mark, and I'm tired. Didn't you eat anything on the plane?"

"Of course I did," he replied sharply. "If you consider a bag of pretzels and a Coke dinner."

"Fine," she answered wearily. "Whatever you want to do."

"Tomorrow's Saturday," I said, trying to help the situation. "We can all sleep late if we want."

"No, we can't," said my mom. "I've made plans for us."

"What plans?" asked my father.

"I'll tell you when we get to the restaurant."

Turning to his friend, my father asked, "How about it, Carlitos? Want to join us for dinner?"

"*Gracias, pero no*, Mark," he said. "I've got to get on the road." Carlos lives in New Braunfels, a small town near San Antonio. "I'll see you Monday morning." They shook hands. Carlos Montoya took my mom's hand and kissed it again. "*Hasta luego, señora* Baron."

After we left the airport, we drove to a nearby restaurant—an open twenty-four hours, hole-in-the-wall place called Lorenzo's Grill. I was a little surprised that my father chose that place. It wasn't the type of restaurant we generally eat at. Perhaps he picked it because it was one of the few restaurants in the area still open, and he was too tired to look for another one. I was also surprised that there were so many customers eating at that hour. The place was alive with loud voices, banging dishes, and clanging metal trays. An old jukebox near the entrance blared out a twangy country and western tune.

A man I guessed to be the manager or the owner or both greeted us. He led us to a red vinyl booth at the back of the restaurant. We sat next to a loud, rowdy party of men and women. With them was a little girl who couldn't have been more than five years old. She had fallen asleep in her chair. At the head of the table sat a fat, bald, man with a thick, grayish, walrus moustache. He was drinking a large stein of beer. The man was telling an apparently hilarious story that made his table convulse with laughter.

"Molly, about your plans for tomorrow, I don't know what you have in mind, but I'd really just like to stay home," said my father, exhaustion from his earlier bout, the plane trip, and the whole week sucking the energy out of his voice. "I've been on the road almost every night for the past month."

My mom sat her menu down. "That's just it, Mark. You hardly ever spend any time with us. I thought we'd do something together as a family for once."

He leaned his head back and closed his eyes. "All right, what did you have in mind?"

She forced a smile. "I spoke with your mother this morning. I've invited your parents to go with us to take Jesse to tour the Alamo tomorrow. He still hasn't seen it. Anyway, we could make a whole day of it. Afterwards, we could have lunch at the Riverwalk, maybe even do some shopping."

" . . . and then he says to me, 'You can't drive through here. This is private property.' And I say, 'Oh, yeah? Watch me!'" The fat man's voice at the table next to us grew louder. "So I give it the gas and . . . WHOOSH! I run my pickup through the gate. Chickens and feathers fly every which way. Ol' Grady's eyeballs pop out of his head like Jackie Gleason's on *The Honeymooners*." The fat man's eyes widened comically. He guffawed hysterically and the others at his table laughed with him.

"Sure, okay, that'll be fine," my father said. "I'll sleep in on Sunday, then."

"I was hoping you'd join us for church on Sunday, Mark."

My father rolled his eyes. "Come on, Molly, you know I've got to leave early Monday morning for the TV tapings in Philadelphia."

She threw her hands up in exasperation. "Oh, what's the use? Can't I get it through your head that we need you here? Jesse needs you!"

"What do you want me to do, Molly? Give up my career? Is that what you want?"

My father kept his voice low so as not to attract attention, unlike the man across from us.

"All right, I'll march into Frank Collins' office on Monday morning and tell him I quit. And after he sues me for breach of contract and we're completely broke . . . "

"Um, pardon me, sir."

My father glanced up. A young waitress with blond hair stood over him.

"Are you . . . ? Oh my gosh, it *is* you!" she squealed. "You're the Angel of Death, aren't you!" She turned around and yelled at the other waitresses, "I told you it was him!"

Three waitresses and the manager-or-owner-or-both instantly surrounded our booth.

"I recognized you even without your face paint," the waitress said. "I told Wanda, 'That's the Angel of Death from ACW over there.' She thought I was crazy, but I knew it was you the minute you walked in. Is this your family? Hi. I absolutely adore your husband," she told my mom. "Oh, don't get me wrong. It's not like that. It's just that I never miss *Monday Night Mayhem*. Of course, I work on Monday nights, but I set my VCR to tape it. Then I watch it as soon as I get home." She whipped out a pen and a slip of paper from her apron. "Could I please have your autograph? My name's Delores." She pointed to her name badge.

My father nodded. "Sure."

He never refuses to sign an autograph for a fan. "They're the reason we're in this business in the first place," he says. My mom, on the other hand, prefers that they just leave us alone. All this unwanted attention was only aggravating the friction between them. She sat there, staring down at the tabletop, seething. She hadn't wanted to come here in the first place. Now all this.

"Listen," said the manager-or-owner-or-both. "Dinner's on the house. Anything you want." He smiled cheerily.

"Thank you," my father said. "But that's not . . . "

The manager-or-owner-or-both snapped his fingers. "Say, I just remembered. I've got a camera in the office.

Hold on, I'll go get it." He dashed off and disappeared through a door behind the counter.

My father signed autographs for the other waitresses.

A moment later, the manager-or-owner-or-both reappeared. "I've got two shots left," he said, waving his camera in the air. "I hope you don't mind. I'd like to take a picture of me and you shaking hands."

"Don't forget about us, Walter," one of the waitresses said. "We want to be in a picture with him, too."

My father rose from the booth and posed for two photographs—one with the manager-or-owner-or-both and the other with the waitresses hanging all over him like they were his girlfriends or something.

By this time the rest of the customers in the restaurant had become our audience. Based on the staff's reaction to my father, they figured he was somebody important, even if they didn't recognize him.

The fat man at the table next to us rose and staggered over. "You're a rassler, ain't you?" His enormous belly hung over his belt, challenging the buttons on his sweat-stained plaid shirt.

"He's the Angel of Death from American Championship Wrestling," the manager-or-owner-or-both said proudly.

The fat man snorted. "That stuff's all fake, ain't it?" he said. "Not like in boxing where boxers really hurt each other. You rasslers dress up in girly tights and dance around the ring like a bunch of ballerinas, play fightin'."

My father ignored him and sat down. The waitresses and the manager-or-owner-or-both returned to their duties, but the fat man remained standing by our booth. He glared at my father.

"Lessee if you can take me in a arm rasslin' contest," he said. His speech was slurred from the beer.

Without looking up, my father said, "Why don't you go back to your table, mister?"

"Whassa matter?" The fat man grinned. His two front teeth were missing, and the others looked like brown tree stumps. "'Fraid I'll beat you?"

He stooped down and plopped his elbow on our table. A whiff of armpit odor wafted in my direction, assaulting my sense of smell.

"C'mon, let's see how strong you really are."

Having gone through similar idiotic challenges throughout his wrestling career, my father was not about to be goaded into some ridiculous display of strength with a man who'd obviously had too much to drink.

"Look, friend," my father said, "I'm sure you can beat me in arm wrestling. But right now, I'm trying to have dinner with my family, okay?"

The man remained hunched over with his elbow on our table. "C'mon, just one time. Lessee what you got."

"Barney!" A woman from the fat man's party called out. "Leave those people alone."

The fat man didn't budge. "I will, as soon as he arm-rassles me!"

"Mark, let's go," said my mom. She'd had more than enough of Lorenzo's Grill, and we still hadn't eaten a thing.

My father readily agreed. "Excuse me, mister, we're leaving." We slid out of the booth.

"I knew it," the fat man growled. "You're a phony!"

"If you say so," my father muttered, unperturbed by the insult.

We headed toward the door. The manager-or-owner-or-both hurried up to us with a worried expression on his face. "I–Is something wrong, sir?" Then it dawned on him. He slapped his head. "Oh, please forgive me, folks. Somebody will take your order right away. I–In fact, I'll do it myself. Please have a seat. Don't forget. It's my treat," he said, reminding us of his earlier offer.

"No, it's not that," my father told him. "It's been a long day and it's late. We need to get home."

"A–Are you sure?" the manager-or-owner-or-both sputtered. "All right, I understand, but please come back soon." He opened the door and let us out.

We headed for our car.

"I'll make you a sandwich when we get home, Mark," my mom said. "And I think we have a can of chicken noodle soup in the pantry."

"Yeah, sure, that'll be fine."

But a sandwich and a bowl of soup are no substitutes for the rib eye steak and baked potato he had talked about ordering.

"Hey!" a voice from the darkness rang out. The fat man and two of his friends were standing outside the restaurant doors. "We know you can fake fight in a rasslin' ring. Lessee what you can do for real." The fat man grinned his broken windows grin. Images of Manny, Chester, and Hugo instantly popped into my head.

My mom spun around. Panic and fear swept through her. "Jesse! Run inside and tell them to call the police!"

"No," said my father with amazing tranquility. "Both of you get in the car."

"But, Dad!" I protested.

"Do what I said," he ordered, never taking his eyes off the men.

Reluctantly, we got in.

From the window I watched the silhouettes of the three men slowly waddle toward our car. I knew my father could easily take on the fat man if he had to. But I didn't know what would happen if he fought all three of them at the same time.

My mom gripped my wrists tightly, terrified of what might happen next. My heart pounded fiercely. Throbbing pain bounced against the walls in my head. Why hadn't we just gone home from the airport like my mom had wanted? And of all the restaurants in San Antonio, why did we have to stop at this seedy place?

My father stepped away from our car. With a menacing scowl on his face, he stretched his six-foot, seven-inch, three-hundred-twenty-pound body to full height. He thrust out his arms, like a gunslinger getting ready to draw.

The men froze momentarily.

"You boys go back inside to your families," he said, in that deep, robot-like, Angel of Death voice. He didn't blink or take his eyes off them.

Inside the restaurant, sitting down, being made a fuss over by the waitresses, my father looked misleadingly disarming. But out in the parking lot, late at night, with his black leather jacket covering his towering, muscular body, his long black hair flowing in the breeze, and the full moon glistening on his face, he looked every bit the part of the Angel of Death, the "emissary from the lower regions of the Netherworld."

"Go on," he commanded in that same ominous tone. He took a single step forward. Nervously, the men retreated back a couple of steps. He continued to stare at them for what seemed an eternity. It was eerie watching him, as if he were hypnotizing them. Finally, without saying another word, the men turned and reentered Lorenzo's Grill. With his eyes still focused on the restaurant doors, my father slowly opened the driver's side of the car and slid in.

He drove off, leaving the men wondering what would have happened had they tangled with the Angel of Death in the Lorenzo's Grill parking lot. I couldn't help wonder what would have happened, too.

CHAPTER NINE

"Wake up, champ."

My father rested his huge hand on my shoulder and nudged me. I cleared the sleep out of my eyes in rapid blinks and glanced up.

"Morning, Dad."

He sat on my bed and brushed my hair out of my face. "Sleep well?"

"Yes," I lied.

When we arrived home last night, I had a hard time falling asleep. At first, it was because I was still pretty worked up about the confrontation at the restaurant. After that, it was my parents' talking that kept me awake. Even with my bedroom door shut, I could hear their voices, which, at times, grew to near shouts.

"How are things at school?" he asked.

"Fine." Another lie.

"Mom told me about your teacher's visit the other day."

I sat up, propping myself on my elbows. "Honest, Dad, things *are* fine," I said, wondering what my mom had told him.

He chuckled. "I'm sure they are. I thought your teacher's visit was pretty funny, to tell you the truth."

"You did?"

"Jesse, wrestling fans will do just about anything they can to meet their favorite superstars."

"I tried to tell Mom that," I said. "My teacher didn't come here because she was worried about me. She came because she wanted to meet *you*. But Mom didn't want to hear any of it. That's why we're going to the Alamo today. Mom thinks going there will help me in my history class."

"Well, it can't hurt," he said. "Besides, you've wanted to see it ever since we moved here. Now you'll have your chance."

He picked up the Angel of Death action figure from my headboard shelf and scrutinized its exaggerated features. He's always thought the toy manufacturers get carried away with adding muscles and ripples on the toys' bodies he knows he doesn't possess.

"Dad, were you really going to fight those guys at the restaurant last night?" It was a question that had haunted me all night.

He laughed. "Jesse, those men didn't want to fight. Not really. They were more interested in trying to scare me." He placed the action figure back on the shelf. "That's usually the case with bullies. They're control freaks. They try to intimidate you into thinking they're tough. But once they see you're not afraid of them, once they lose control of the situation, they generally back off. Anyway, I could sense that they had more bark in them than bite. More beer, too," he added with a smile.

I wasn't sure what to make of what he said. I don't know if Manny and Chester and Hugo would back away from me, no matter how much bravery I displayed. I sure hadn't scared them off the other day.

There was another question that had been bothering me. But up until now, I hadn't had the nerve to ask him or my mom.

"Dad, are you and Mom going to get divorced?" The question slipped out of my mouth before I had a chance to think about whether or not I wanted to ask it.

"What?" He sat up straight. "Is that what you think, Jesse?"

I pulled myself out of the covers and sat next to him. "It's just that you and Mom argue a lot, Dad, and . . . well, she left you once before. I–I'm not sure what to think."

He wrapped a heavy arm around me and kissed me on the top of my head. He hadn't kissed me since I was maybe in the second grade.

"Jesse, a wrestling career is strenuous on any marriage. Being on the road is just as difficult for me as it is for you and Mom. I wish things were better, champ, I really do. But to answer your question, Jesse—no, Mom and I are not going to get divorced. I love her and you more than anything in the world, and I'm not going to lose what I've got."

It sounded strange hearing him say he loved me. I mean, I know he does. After all, he *is* my father. But he never actually tells me he loves me. I guess he just assumes I know. Still, it'd be nice if he said it more often, for no special reason.

"I'll let you in on a little secret, though," my father continued. "*All* couples argue. For a million different reasons. The barber argues with his wife. The lady at the checkout counter at the grocery store argues with her husband. We all have disagreements of one kind or another. That's life. Anyway, I don't plan to continue wrestling much longer."

I gazed at him, confused. "You don't?"

"I've had a great career, Jesse. And despite the problems that go with it, I wouldn't trade my job for anything else. Still, I'm not getting any younger, and my knees are pretty banged up. There's a year and a half left in my contract that I've got to honor. But after that . . . we'll see." He shrugged. "I'll let you in on another little secret," he added, smiling. "The Angel of Death is going to meet with a 'serious accident' at *The Final Stand.*"

"You're dropping the belt to Prince Romulus?" I asked, shocked at the thought.

"Are you kidding? Half the locker room would pitch a fit if Frank Collins allowed that to happen."

I didn't doubt that for a second. Most wrestlers backstage don't think the Prince has been in the business long enough to represent the ACW as its champion. The only reason the promoters have given him a title match is to offer my father a different type of opponent than the usual contenders for the belt. Also while Prince Romulus may not be ready to be the next ACW heavyweight champ, he does put on a terrific performance in the ring.

Prince Romulus isn't really a prince. Nor is his name Romulus. His real name is Scott Blanchard, and he's originally from Detroit. But on American Championship Wrestling, he's Prince Romulus, the nephew of Il Gran Mephisto, a wealthy tycoon from the island of Sardinia. Except that he's not related to Il Gran Mephisto, either. And Il Gran Mephisto's not really a wealthy tycoon from Sardinia. Outside of the ring, Mephisto is Joe Di Paolo from Topeka, Kansas.

Il Gran Mephisto used to be a top wrestler for the ACW, but neck injuries forced him to retire a couple of years ago. Rather than having him leave the business, Frank Collins offered him a job as a manager.

That's when Scott Blanchard, a wrestler from the independent circuit, was brought in. He was given the gimmick of Prince Romulus, Mephisto's nephew.

Il Gran Mephisto accompanies Prince Romulus to the ring for each match. His primary purpose is to rile the audience, have them boo and shout disparaging words. He also distracts the referee in order to allow the Prince to commit all sorts of heinous rule-breaking tactics—eye gouging, biting, choking—while the referee's back is turned.

One of the coolest things about Il Gran Mephisto is that he can shoot flames from his fingers. Actually, he can't really shoot fire. It's done with "flash paper," a chemically treated material often used by magicians in their acts.

At a certain point during the match, when Prince Romulus's opponents are getting the upper hand, Mephisto whips out the flash paper and a cigarette lighter he's secretly hidden in his coat. With sleight of hand, he ignites the special paper and flings a ball of "fire" into their faces. Romulus's opponents fall down, writhing in pain from the "burns" they've suffered.

No one is hurt, of course. But that's only because, like with all high-risk wrestling maneuvers, Il Gran Mephisto has practiced this trick a million times, under safe conditions.

Yet, despite all his colorfulness, Prince Romulus is not what ACW officials consider championship material. For one thing, he doesn't have the size that they look for in a champion. Frank Collins prefers larger men as holders of the heavyweight belt. Also, in the opinion of the ACW, he lacks charisma. They feel he's weak on the microphone. That's one of the reasons they paired him up with Il Gran

Mephisto. Mephisto, an old veteran of the business, does all the talking for him. He delivers some of the best interviews I've ever heard.

"We still haven't worked out all the details yet, but I can tell you this much, Jesse," said my father. "After the pay-per-view, the Angel of Death will spend the next four weeks out of the ring 'rehabilitating' from injuries suffered during his match. I'm going to do my best to make up for lost time with you and Mom."

"Dad, are you serious?" I couldn't believe it!

"As serious as a toothache, champ." He patted me on the shoulder. "Get yourself ready. Your *güelos* will be here shortly. Then let's go out and enjoy the day."

"Will your injury in the match involve Il Gran Mephisto's fire?" I asked.

"You never know," he said with a wry smile as he left my room.

Unlike other sports, professional wrestling is not seasonal. Wrestlers perform all year long. The wrestling business doesn't come with built-in vacations like most jobs, either. Often, when a wrestling superstar needs time off — usually to get some rest, but sometimes to undergo surgery to repair old injuries — Frank Collins and his team of writers work it into their story lines.

For example, a couple of summers ago, my father took a few weeks off from the ring. That was the time we drove to the Grand Canyon. At the time, the Angel of Death and Butcher Murdock were tag-team partners. The writers came up with a story line that called for my father to accidentally clothesline Murdock during a match against the Midnight Raiders. Murdock retaliated. The Angel of Death and Butcher Murdock then viciously fought each other, eventually getting disqualified. Later that evening,

Murdock ambushed my father in the dressing room with a metal pipe, leaving him bleeding and unconscious. The paramedics were called in. They carried the Angel of Death away in a gurney to a waiting ambulance. It was horrifying to watch on TV.

Except that I knew it was all an act. I knew he wasn't hurt at all. My father had warned my mom and me about what would happen beforehand. Don Murdock and my father were, and still are, good friends. The attack, however, helped explain the Angel of Death's absence from television for the next several weeks.

The funny thing about that incident is that the ACW received hundreds of cards and letters from fans, wishing the Angel of Death a speedy recovery. They also urged him to get revenge on Murdock.

But as we stood taking in the magnificent, breathtaking beauty of the Grand Canyon, the last thing on my father's mind was seeking revenge on his good friend Butcher Murdock.

Now that I think about it, that was the last vacation we took together.

About an hour later, my grandparents arrived.

"*¿Cómo estás, Jesse?*" my grandmother greeted me.

"Fine, Güela," I said. "How are you?"

She turned to my father and complained, "*Ay, Marcos, ¿Cuándo le vas enseñar español a este muchacho?*"

"He knows how to speak Spanish, Ma," replied my father. He winked at me and said, "Jesse, tell Güela how to say 'four men in quicksand' in Spanish."

"Cuatro Sinko," I said. Sara had told me that joke, and I'd been repeating it to everyone I knew.

Everybody laughed, except Güela.

The Alamo sits in the middle of downtown San Antonio surrounded by shops, restaurants, and hotels. To be honest with you, at first sight, I was a little disappointed.

The Alamo is not nearly as big as I thought it would be. It's also hard to imagine that this is the battleground where, for thirteen days, two hundred or so Texans fought against an army of almost five thousand Mexican soldiers. But there it stood — a proud, dignified symbol of Texas independence.

We entered the Alamo. Inside, people spoke in hushed tones, out of respect for the old mission, as well as for all the men who died in it.

All the stuff Mrs. Petrosky had talked about in class suddenly came alive for me. As I studied the artifacts encased in glass cases, the names Travis, Crockett, and Bowie had new relevance. I thought of all the men who chose to remain here to fight, even against insurmountable odds, ultimately dying for their noble cause. I also felt sorry for all the Mexican soldiers who marched all the way from Mexico in the cold winter, only to die here under orders from a cruel and unmerciful dictator.

Walking around, I noticed some of the visitors pointing at my father and whispering. *Oh, no,* I thought. *He's been spotted.* No one approached him, though. Not until we stepped outside.

"Jesse, stand in front of the Alamo next to your *papi*," said Güelo, aiming his camera at us.

Before he had a chance to snap a picture, a man and a woman with two little kids approached us.

"You're the Angel of Death from ACW, aren't you?" said the man.

My father smiled. "Yes, I am."

"Is it all right if my wife takes a picture of you and me together?"

"Sure."

The man, wearing an I ♥ SAN ANTONIO T-shirt and a pair of khaki shorts, stood next to him. He placed one arm around my father's shoulders and shook hands with him with the other, as if he and my father were best friends.

"Young man, please move," the man's wife said, shooing me with her hand. "I'm trying to take a picture."

Embarrassed, I slipped out of the way.

After his wife snapped the photo, she handed him the camera, and he took a picture of her and my father. Then another one of my father with the kids.

Other fans flocked around him. It was almost as if they had been waiting to make sure my father really was the Angel of Death and not just someone who resembled him.

It reminded me of the time when I was little and my mom had taken me to the mall. While she was trying on clothes, I played in the dress racks. I used to love running my face through all that fabric. As I poked my head through a wall of clothes, I saw my mom coming toward me. Quickly, I hid among the dresses. When she was right in front of me, I leaped out and grabbed her. Only it wasn't my mom. A lady wearing a skirt similar to hers screamed and jumped about two feet in the air. She lost her balance and fell against a dress rack.

I never mistook someone else for my mom after that.

I stood over to the side with my mom and my grandparents. Together, we watched the frenzy. There were more photos taken—dozens and dozens, it seemed like.

Pens and slips of paper were shoved in my father's face. And he signed each one of them.

A little boy asked him to show him his muscles. My father raised his arms and flexed his enormous biceps. The kid hung from my father's arm like it was a playground jungle gym.

I know this is silly, but I had a strange urge to knock that kid down and say to him, "That's my dad! Why don't you go play with your own?" For a split second, I wanted to run over there and climb up his arm, maybe have him lift me onto his shoulders like he used to. But that's stupid. I'm in the seventh grade. Still, I didn't like it that my father was playing around with some other kid.

This morning, he had assured me that we were going to have a fun day. This was supposed to be a family outing. It was a family outing all right. My father with everyone else's family.

The little boy punched him in the stomach as hard as he could. My father doubled over, pretending to be hurt, then straightened up and smiled. He tousled the kid's hair.

"Is it always like this, m'ija?" Güela asked with concern.

My mom nodded and groaned, "Always."

"Don't be so hard on him, Molly," Güelo told her. "It's part of his job. He's representing the company he works for."

"I realize that, I guess. But there are times when I wish he had a job that didn't bring so much attention to him or to us."

My grandfather hugged her. "M'ija," he said, "God didn't make Marcos that size so he could sit behind a desk. He's doing what he was meant to do."

I watched as some teenage girls flirted with my father. The little boy tried to climb up his arms again. More people approached him for his autograph. Cameras continued to flash.

Is that what he was meant to do? Spend Saturday afternoons hanging out with a bunch of strangers instead of with his family? People he didn't know? People he'd probably never see again?

Although I'd experienced this time and time again, the things he and my mom had been arguing about suddenly became clear to me. It was as if a veil had been lifted from my face, and I was seeing him in a new light. Despite what he'd told me earlier, I realized now that he would never stop being the Angel of Death. He loved it too much.

After he underwent his third knee operation a year ago, he swore he was going to retire then. But as soon as his knee got better, he returned to the ring, against my mom's wishes.

"Mark, you're thirty-eight years old, and you've got the legs of an old man," she had told him. "You're going to wind up crippled for life if you continue wrestling!"

Watching those people fawning over him, all that adoring adulation, I could understand why it would be difficult to give up being the Angel of Death. But what about us? Where did we fit in the picture?

My mind flashed back to all the important events in my life he'd missed out on—birthday parties, school programs, Christmases that had to be celebrated before or after the 25th because of scheduling conflicts. Even today. I'd been dumped—replaced by a bunch of nerdy wrestling fans.

The little boy squealed with delight as my dad lifted him and sat him on his shoulders. The teenage girls oohed and aahed as they touched his muscles.

I felt a thick lump grow in my throat. My eyes began to sting with tears as a sad realization sank in. *You don't love me. That's why you can't ever say it. They're the ones you really love.*

I glanced over at my mom. She sat on the ground, angrily tearing out blades of grass.

I don't know if my father really believed they couldn't possibly get divorced or if he had simply told me that to soothe my fears.

My grandparents sat patiently on a bench, waiting for the scene to play itself out. If Güelo didn't notice the tension between my parents, Güela certainly did. Her wrinkled face filled with anguish as she swiveled her head from my mother to my father.

As the kid cheerfully bounced up and down on my father's shoulders, I thought, *I hope you fall!*

CHAPTER TEN

On Sunday morning we attended my grandparents' church. Although he didn't say anything about it, I knew my father had agreed to go as a way of making up for the ruined trip to the Alamo the day before. I didn't particularly want to go either, since the service was in Spanish.

But I didn't need to be a fluent Spanish speaker to understand that the pastor, Reverend Dominguez, was giving my father the "star" treatment. During the welcome, he had him stand. Then he rattled off something about *lucha libre*. I knew that had to do with professional wrestling because I'd heard Carlos Montoya say it when he talked about the time he wrestled in Mexico. When the pastor finished, the congregation applauded enthusiastically. That wouldn't have been so bad if they had also clapped for the other visitors as well. But they were basically ignored.

The rest of the service was pretty incomprehensible, although I managed to catch a phrase here and there that I understood.

After his message was over, Reverend Dominguez extended an invitation of prayer. My mom rose and walked down the aisle. She dropped to her knees at the altar to pray. Soon, Güela accompanied her.

Even through the pastor's booming voice, the piano and organ music, and the congregation singing, I could hear them sobbing. I wanted to go to them, join them in prayer, but I felt awkward doing so. My father sat next to me, his head buried in his hymnal, singing softly. I felt like I would be abandoning him, taking sides, if I went forward.

Instead, I sat there and tried to pray in my head. I wasn't sure if that would be acceptable to God. Did I have to say the words aloud in order for Him to hear my prayer? Or could God read my mind and know my thoughts? I decided that since God can do anything, He'd know what I was thinking. So in my head I prayed, *Dear God, please don't let my parents fight so much. And please don't let them get divorced.*

When the service was over, as expected, autograph hounds mobbed my father outside the church. He signed church bulletins and even a Bible.

After that, we drove to my grandparents' house for lunch.

We were met at the steps by Pollo, a light brown, mixed Labrador. My grandfather named him Pollo, which means chicken in Spanish, because as a puppy, he was terrified of their cat, Gremlin. Even though Pollo has now grown to three times the size of Gremlin, he still stays out of the cat's way whenever it walks past him.

Inside their house, the walls, much like ours, were covered with wrestling memorabilia. There were photos of my father in various stages of his career, from his Mangler and Annihilator days, to his current persona. Mrs. Petrosky would be in wrestling fan heaven if she saw all this.

Lunch was *carne guisada*, a type of beef stew, with rice, beans, and tortillas.

While we ate, my grandparents reminisced about the days when my father was young.

"He was always big for his age," said Güelo. "That's why the coaches at his school got him involved in football."

"*Sí*, but that's also when he stopped taking piano lessons," Güela lamented.

I looked at my father, astonished. "I didn't know you play the piano."

He smiled. "I don't, champ. Not really."

"Of course you do," said Güela. "Don't let him fool you, Jesse. Your *papi* plays quite well. Did you know he also plays the guitar?"

"Ma, don't start with that," said my father, now blushing.

"When he was in high school, he and his friends formed one of those rock and roll bands," she said. "They used to practice in the garage, singing and playing night after night."

My father broke out laughing. "Ma, we were horrible."

"*They* were horrible," Güela said. "Especially that *muchacho* with the long, wild hair. When he sang, he sounded like someone was killing a pig!"

Everyone laughed.

"But you were good, Marcos. You were the only talented one in the bunch." My grandmother pushed her chair back from the table and imitated playing a guitar. "His fingers moved so fast, they were just a blur."

"Don't exaggerate, Ma," said my father, chuckling.

My mom smiled. "You *did* play the guitar. I'd almost forgotten that. In fact, that's one of the things that I found attractive about you."

"You mean it wasn't the football uniform or the way I sacked quarterbacks?" my father joked.

She turned to me. "Jesse, all through college, your father used to carry his guitar case around with him. We'd sit under a tree on the university campus, and he'd play some of the most beautiful love songs."

"What happened to your guitar?" I asked.

My father sighed. "Money was pretty tight in those days, champ. So I sold it to one of the guys on the team who wanted to learn how to play the guitar."

"But we still have the piano," said my grandmother. "Marcos, after we finish eating, I want you to play something for us."

"It's been a long time, Ma," my father said. "I'm not sure I can play anything anymore."

"Of course you can," she insisted. "Music is a natural talent for you."

After lunch, my mom and grandmother cleared the table. Güelo and I sat on the couch. He leafed through the Sunday newspaper while I read the comics page. My father sat at the piano—an old, black, upright Wurlitzer. He played a few chords, just a warm-up. But I was surprised he had that much skill. I never knew he was musical.

A few moments later, my mom and Güela joined us.

"Play that song you wrote for me, Mark," said my mom.

My father looked puzzled. "What song?"

"The song that made me fall in love with you."

"Dad wrote a song for you?" I asked. I was amazed by all this new information. He played the guitar and the piano. And he composed songs, too. Funny, but all my life I'd never thought of him as anything but a wrestler.

"Dad wrote lots of songs," said my mom. "He was also a great poet."

"Just a lot of silly words," muttered my father, brushing off the compliment.

My mom rose from the couch and wrapped her arms around his neck. "Sing *La dueña de mi amor,* Mark. For me."

This was the most affection she'd shown him in a while. I glanced at my *güela.* She seemed to be pleading with her eyes, hoping he wouldn't refuse.

"*Ándale,* Marcos," she coaxed. "Play that beautiful song."

My father began to play. Then he sang. "*A la dueña de mi amor, estos versos le dedico. Si encuentran algún error, que me perdonen, lo suplico.*

"*Nací, mujer, para adorarte. Y perdona si al cantarte lloro. Mi único placer es contemplarte, porque yo de corazón te adoro.*"

I don't know what he was singing, but it made my mom swoon. She closed her eyes and swayed with the tune. My grandmother's eyes glistened. My grandfather, completely oblivious to the music, continued reading the newspaper.

My father ended with "*Por eso, noche y día yo me siento con orgullo. Porque dices que eres mía, y yo te digo que soy tuyo.*"

When he finished, they kissed. They kissed for a long time.

I don't know if God was answering my prayer, but it was a good start.

CHAPTER ELEVEN

On Monday morning, I handed Mrs. Petrosky her autographed picture of the Angel of Death, along with her autograph book. She hugged me tightly, smothering me in her brown wool sweater. It was embarrassing to be hugged that way by my teacher in front of the class. But I didn't pull away. I didn't want to chance hurting her feelings.

"Who is your father going to wrestle tonight, Jesse?" she asked excitedly.

"I'm not sure," I said.

That was true. My father seldom speaks about his matches. He goes out and does his job, much like everyone else. Except that he beats people up for a living. When he does talk about wrestling, he usually tells funny stories about the "boys." That's how he refers to his fellow wrestlers.

There was the time, for instance, when Ice Man Jacob Sloane, who is an amateur magician, was showing the boys backstage a trick he'd recently learned. He had Red Lassiter handcuff him, hands behind his back, to a metal pole. Sloane bragged that he could uncuff himself in less than fifteen seconds.

But after fifteen seconds, he still couldn't get free. He tugged and twisted, but the handcuffs wouldn't open. Minutes later, while the other wrestlers hooted and howled with laughter, Jacob Sloane sent Red Lassiter to get the key for the handcuffs from his dressing room. Lassiter searched everywhere, turning Sloane's dressing room upside down, but he couldn't find the key anywhere.

Sloane and Lassiter were scheduled to fight against the Black Mamba and Dr. Inferno, and their match was up next.

While Sloane struggled to get loose, Frank Collins ordered his crew to find a pair of wire cutters. In the meantime, he quickly put together a match between Wally Armstrong, who wasn't even scheduled to fight that night, and Gargoyle Gorman, who'd wrestled in an earlier bout.

The ring announcer, Dan Greenberg, introduced it as a "bonus match." But the live audience wasn't interested in watching two jobbers fight. They booed loudly. They chanted, "Bo-rring! Bo-rring!" as Gargoyle Gorman and Wally Armstrong kept their match going, stalling for time.

Finally, in an instinctive act of pure genius, Frank Collins created a scenario in which the cameras showed Red Lassiter frantically searching for his tag-team partner. He found Sloane "badly beaten" and handcuffed to a pole, purportedly the dastardly work of the Black Mamba and Dr. Inferno. Seconds later, in a TV interview, Red Lassiter vowed revenge against his partner's attackers. He recruited Kronos to team up with him to avenge the vicious beating of the Ice Man.

The match was pretty decent with a tremendous effort on everyone's part, considering it had been put together so quickly.

While the show was still in progress and since wire cutters or the key still hadn't been located, a crew member rushed out of the arena and found a hardware store nearby. He quickly purchased a hacksaw and speeded back.

Jacob Sloane's handcuffs were finally off. He ran down to ringside before the match was over and helped Red Lassiter and Kronos defeat their opponents, at the same time getting revenge for his "attack."

Although no one ever found out, Carlos Montoya later admitted to my father that he had taken Jacob Sloane's key. He'd also slightly bent some of the teeth on the handcuffs so that Sloane wouldn't be able to undo them easily. Carlos has never liked Sloane. He doesn't care for Sloane's arrogant attitude backstage toward the younger, less experienced wrestlers. Ice Man Jacob Sloane plays a face on TV, but backstage, he's not very well liked by the boys.

Mrs. Petrosky took down a framed photograph of her dog, a brown pug wearing a pink bonnet, from the wall next to her desk. She replaced her dog's picture with my father's, then hung it back up.

"Do you think you might be able to get me one of those, too?" Wendell asked hopefully, as he emptied his backpack and stuffed his books inside his desk.

"That picture already belonged to Mrs. Petrosky," I explained. "I had my father autograph it for her, that's all."

"Kissing up to the teacher, dork?"

Oh, no. I turned around. Manny Alvarez, Hugo Sanchez, and Chester Leonard were standing behind me. This was their first day back from their suspension.

Ignoring them, I sat down and pulled out my history book.

Manny leaned over. He whispered in my ear, "See you at the blacktop . . . hero!"

I sat there stunned. I was hoping Manny had forgotten about the other day. Or maybe he'd decided another suspension wouldn't be worth it.

What was I going to do? I didn't want to fight him. I'd probably get suspended, too, not to mention getting a busted nose or a black eye. I dreaded to think how my mom would react if that happened.

I glanced over at Wendell. I wondered if he'd be any help if the three of them started beating me up. If I weren't so nervous, I'd laugh. Poor Wendell couldn't beat a drum. Maybe the other guys would jump in—Goose, Terrance, and some of the others. They'd been so anxious to be my friends. Could I count on them now? I didn't think so. I couldn't blame them, really.

I could let Coach Johnson know about Manny. He was already aware of the situation. But how could I live that down later? Everybody would know I snitched. They'd accuse me of being a chicken.

After visiting the Alamo, I had actually looked forward to coming to class. I was beginning to find Texas history a fascinating subject. But it was almost impossible to concentrate on what Mrs. Petrosky was saying. I could feel Manny's hot breath in my ear saying, *See you at the blacktop . . . hero.*

When Texas history was over, we filed out of the room for our next class. Manny purposely bumped me as he passed by. I ignored him, which by doing so, I'm sure I only verified his belief that I was scared of him.

Out in the hall Wendell said, "Cody says he saw your dad outside your house. Is he still in town? 'Cause if he is, maybe we could come over after school to meet him."

I started to tell Wendell that I had no idea who Cody was. Instead I said, "My father was here this past weekend, but he's gone now. He's wrestling tonight."

Wendell's face sank. "Well, when will he be back?"

"I don't know."

We headed down the hall. Finally Wendell blasted me. "If you don't want us to meet your dad, why don't you just say so?"

"Wendell, it's not that."

"Look, Jesse, I've tried to be friends with you, but you act like you're too good for us. Well, maybe your dad's a hotshot wrestler, but you're not. You're just a kid like everybody else at this school."

"I'm not lying, Wendell! I really don't know when my father's going to be home. You watch ACW every Monday night, don't you? They give a schedule of upcoming wrestling appearances during the show. Baton Rouge one night, Atlanta the next, Jacksonville the night after. Maybe *your* father comes home from work every evening, but mine doesn't, okay?"

Wendell grew silent. Then he said, "I don't have a father."

"What do you mean, you don't . . . "

"My parents are divorced."

His words knocked the wind out of me. "Wendell, I–I'm sorry. I didn't know."

He shrugged. "That's all right. They've been divorced for a while."

"But you still have a father," I said, trying to smooth my blunder. "Even if your parents are divorced."

Wendell lowered his eyes and stared at the floor. He kicked a wadded gum wrapper someone had carelessly dropped and sent it skidding across the hallway. "No, I don't. Not really. My dad hasn't come around, not even once since he left us almost four years ago. He's never written or called or anything. So as far as I'm concerned, I don't have a father."

"What happened? I don't mean to pry in your business, Wendell, but why'd your parents get divorced?"

Wendell hesitated. He glanced around the hallway, checking to see if anyone was listening to our conversation. Talking about it probably made him uncomfortable. But I wanted to know. I *had* to know.

"Did your parents fight a lot?"

"No. That's the weird thing about it. They never argued at all. At least not that I can recall. One day he just packed his stuff and moved out."

"But there had to be a reason they split up," I persisted.

"I'm sure there was. But every time I ask my mom, the only thing she says is, 'It was your father's choice.' She won't give me any more information than that."

"And you never heard them have any disagreements, arguments of any kind?"

All couples argue, I heard my father say in my mind.

"I wish I had," said Wendell. "That way I'd have had some clue as to why he moved out." His eyes became misty. "Sometimes . . . I think he left because of me."

"Because of you? Why?"

"You know, 'cause . . . I'm kinda fat." He wiped his eyes with the back of his palm.

"Wendell, your being . . . *heavy* didn't have anything to do with your parents' divorce." I couldn't bring myself to say the word "fat."

"I don't know about that," he said. "I think my dad was disappointed he had such a fat kid for a son. He wanted me to be more athletic, like him. He used to work out in a gym all the time. But my mom's a big lady. I guess I got my size from her side of the family. Maybe he decided he didn't like being married to a fat lady with a fat kid anymore."

"No, Wendell, for whatever reason your parents divorced, it wasn't because of that," I said.

"I guess I'll never know, will I?" He took another swipe at his eyes. "I think that if my parents had argued about the problems they were having, there's a chance they wouldn't have gotten divorced," said Wendell. "I mean, as long as people argue, they're at least talking things out, bringing their issues out in the open. But if they never say what's bothering them, how are they supposed to resolve their differences?"

That made sense. I knew why my parents fought. I didn't want them to get divorced, but if they did, at least I'd know the reasons for it. Hopefully, though, they would be able to talk their way through their problems.

It dawned on me that I didn't know anything about Wendell Cooley. I'd never even tried to get to know him or anyone else at school. Over the years I'd grown so accustomed to distancing myself from my classmates. I figured they just wanted to be my friend because of my father. But, had I ever made any real effort to get to know them? Maybe that's why I felt I didn't have any friends.

I had an idea.

"Listen, Wendell, why don't you and the guys come over to my house tonight to watch *Monday Night Mayhem*. My father won't be there, of course, but we have a lot of interesting wrestling stuff that I think you'd enjoy looking at."

Wendell's face brightened. "Really? Yeah, sure, that'll be cool! I'll tell the others, okay?" He bounded off to his next class like a happy puppy.

I'm not sure what made me do that. I'd like to believe I did it because I wanted Wendell to know I appreciated him, even if his father didn't. But perhaps, subconsciously, I did it for a more selfish reason. Maybe I was trying to strengthen my support group in case I needed them when I confronted Manny at the blacktop.

Of course, the real person I wanted to invite over was Sara Young. But her parents didn't allow her to watch wrestling. If they found out she'd watched it at my house, she might get in trouble. I didn't want to chance doing anything that might hurt her, especially after what I'd put her through with Mr. Gillette.

The rest of the morning flew by quickly. I don't remember much of what any of my teachers talked about. My mind was focused solely on Manny Alvarez and Thing One and Thing Two. Maybe he'd just bad-mouth me in front of everybody or insult my father or something. I could deal with that. On the other hand, what if he pounced on me, knocked me to the ground, and started swinging? What if Sara watched it happen? That would be worse than any beating Manny could dish out.

. . . When the stars threw down their spears
And water'd heaven with their tears,
Did he smile his work to see?
Did he who made the lamb make thee?

"Who is the "he" to whom Blake is referring, Mr. Baron?"

Mr. Gillette's voice startled me. "I–I'm sorry, sir. Could you repeat the question?"

He rose from his desk and walked toward mine. He folded his arms across his chest and frowned. "In his poem, 'The Tyger,' who is the 'he' to whom William Blake is referring?"

"I'm not sure, sir," I replied.

Mr. Gillette grabbed my literature book from the top of my desk. He opened it and flipped the pages. "It would help if you followed along with us, Mr. Baron." He slammed the open book down on my desk. With a huff, he headed back down the aisle and took his seat on top of his desk.

Sara turned to me. She flashed a dimpled smile and winked. Without a doubt, she had to be the most beautiful girl I'd ever met.

When the bell rang for our next class, we headed out the door.

"It would help if you followed along with us, Mr. Baron," Sara said in a deep voice, imitating our teacher. She laughed affectionately.

"Mr. Gillette's not so bad," I told her. "I've had worse. Oh, by the way, I have something for you."

"What is it? Flowers? Diamonds?" Sara teased.

I sat my backpack down against the wall, out of the way from the kids who were changing classes. Unzipping a side pocket, I brought out a manila folder.

"Here you go." I handed her a 5 x 7 photograph of the Angel of Death. It didn't have the colorful graphics of the other one nor was it as large, but it was a full-size view of my father.

"He's awesome!" she gushed. "I can't believe this is your dad."

"Of course he is," I said with a smile. "Don't you see the resemblance?"

Sara laughed. "Now that you mention it, you look exactly alike—the same skeleton face, the same long, black hair—you're the spitting image of your father."

I flung my backpack across my shoulders. "I hope you like it."

"I love it, Jesse. Thank you for thinking about me."

Thinking about you? You're never out of my thoughts.

"By the way, I know your parents don't like for you to watch wrestling, but if you happen to be channel surfing tonight around nine o'clock, and you happen to stop on channel 36 for a moment or two, you might just be able to catch a glimpse of my father."

"I'll look out for him," she promised. "See you at lunch."

Lunch! For a moment, I'd forgotten about Manny. I still hadn't figured out what I was going to do about him. As I headed toward my math class, I realized I had about an hour to come up with an answer.

CHAPTER TWELVE

Ever since I met Sara, I'd been dying to eat lunch with her. But she was always surrounded by a bunch of girls. The only time I got to spend with her was a few brief moments on the blacktop after we'd eaten. Maybe I could meet up with her after school, and we could walk home together again. That is, if I'd be able to walk at all after Manny got through with me.

Across the cafeteria, I spotted him. He was sitting with Chester and Hugo and some other thugs. They were laughing about something. Perhaps they were having such a great time, he'd forget about his threat against me.

To my horror, Manny turned and stared in my direction. Everyone at his table turned and stared at me, too. They were still laughing. It seemed I was the source of their amusement.

"Wendy told us you've invited us over to your house tonight to watch wrestling," said Goose. He sat his lunch tray down next to mine. A french fry hung out of the corner of his mouth like a cigarette.

"Yeah, sure," I said, diverting my eyes away from Manny's table.

"Me, too?" asked Terrance.

"Of course."

"What about me?" asked a redheaded kid with braces.

"I don't even know who you are," I said.

"I'm Ronnie Brisco," he replied, grinning a mouth full of metal. "I'm in art class with Wendell."

The conversation drifted off into tonight's show as well as the upcoming pay-per-view event.

"My mom said that if I pass my science test, she'll order *The Final Stand* for Sunday night," said Wendell. "You're all welcome to come over and watch it if you want."

"Me, too?" asked Terrance.

"Yeah, sure," said Wendell.

"What about me?" asked the redheaded kid with braces.

When they finished eating, Manny and his gang rose from their table. They dropped their food trays in the dishwashing area. Then they headed toward us.

"We'll be waiting for you behind the gym," growled Manny. He shoved my chair, squishing me against the table.

"What was that all about?" Wendell asked.

"I, um, think that . . . Manny and them . . . want to beat me up or something," I mumbled.

This was the part where all the guys at my table were supposed to jump in and say something like, "Don't worry, Jesse. You're our friend. We won't let anything happen to you. We'll take care of those punks for you."

But no such luck.

Goose said, "Those guys are tough, man. I wouldn't wanna mess with them."

"Me either," said Terrance. "One time they beat up Rudy Wilkinson because he wouldn't let them borrow his CD player. They busted up Rudy's CD player *and* Rudy. He was absent for almost a week."

"What are you going to do?" asked Wendell.

"You could just sit here until lunch is over," suggested Goose.

I shook my head. "I'll have to face him sometime. I'll see what Manny wants."

We put away our trays and headed out to the blacktop.

The gym is situated at the end of the school building. The back of it faces the teachers' parking lot. Because it is shielded from the view of the rest of the campus, it's difficult for teachers to see what goes on back there. Coach Johnson and Mr. Dennison, one of the assistant principals, patrol the area regularly. My only hope seemed to rest on one of them being there.

Reluctantly, I made my way to the back of the gym. Goose, Terrance, Wendell, and the others trailed behind, keeping a safe distance from me.

Leaning against the wall, in the shade of the noon sun, stood Manny, Chester, and Hugo. Along with them were three other guys, including a boy named Adrian Garcia. Adrian had befriended me on my first day of school. We'd talked about wrestling and other stuff. I thought he was a pretty cool guy, and we got along fine. But I guess he decided it was cooler to hang out with Manny than with me.

When we arrived, Manny glowered at me. "I didn't think you were gonna show up, dork. I thought we were gonna have to go after you." His gang laughed.

"What do you want?" I asked.

"What do I want?" Manny roared. "I told you not to mess with us, didn't I? But you wanted to play the hero, didn't you? Thought you'd impress the little girls."

I glanced over my shoulder. The guys were standing about five yards behind me. They didn't look like they were going to make any attempt to take my side. They were here to watch the onslaught, not unlike the spectators who pay to watch my father fight. Neither Coach Johnson nor Mr. Dennison was anywhere in sight.

I was going to have to fight alone.

Bullies are control freaks. They try to intimidate you into thinking that they're tough. But once they see you're not afraid of them, once they lose control of the situation, they generally back off.

"Let's see what you got, dork," said Manny. He gave me a hard shove.

To everyone's surprise, I shoved him back, sending him stumbling. Hugo and Chester instantly flew to his side.

Take control of the situation.

"You want to fight me?" I yelled at Manny. "Fine, let's do it! But it'll be just you and me. No one else. If Chester or Hugo or anybody else jumps in, then you'll be telling everyone here that you can't beat me by yourself, that you're not tough enough."

"Oh, I'm tough enough to handle you, dork," Manny replied.

Once they lose control of the situation, they generally back off.

"And to make sure no one interferes—from either side—" I said, peering behind me. Not that I thought anyone from my side would jump in. "I want everyone to leave. All of you wait in the front of the gym for us until this is over."

Control the situation.

Manny suddenly seemed unsure of himself. Evidently, no one had ever spoken to him like this before.

"Go on!" I commanded. "Get out of here. All of you. It'll be just Manny and me."

Manny turned to his goons. They stared blankly at him.

"What do you say, Manny?" I said, with growing confidence. "Just you and me. By ourselves. Let's see what *you've* got."

To be honest with you, I didn't know if I could take him. But we were about the same size and weight. I also figured that without his audience to cheer him on, he wouldn't be so cocky, so bold.

Manny's face twisted itself into what looked like . . . fear?

"I–It's some kind of trick," he said, his voice quavering. "That's it, isn't it. You wanna pull some weird wrestling stuff on me and you don't want anybody to see you do it!" Turning to his gang, he told them, "You guys stay where you are."

"No trick, Manny," I said in a mild voice. "Just me. Alone." I grinned impishly, hopefully giving everyone the impression that, indeed, it *was* a trick. That I *was* laying out a trap for Manny.

"You think you're so smart, don't you!" cried Manny. "Well, I'm not about to fall for your stupid tricks." He turned to his goons. "*Vámonos.*" Then to me, he shot a warning: "We'll do this another time."

They retreated to the blacktop, looking for all intents and purposes like a defeated army.

Somehow I got the feeling that there wouldn't be "another time."

The guys on my side went bananas. They whooped and cheered ecstatically. Wendell slapped me on the back. "That has got to be the coolest thing I've ever seen!"

"You got some nerves, man!" said Terrance.

"No fear!" added Goose.

I couldn't speak. My throat had gone completely dry. I glanced down at my pants. I checked to see if I'd wet myself.

CHAPTER THIRTEEN

"How would you like to go to New York?" my mom asked when I got home from school.

"New York?" I tossed my backpack on the recliner and joined her on the couch.

"I spoke to Dad earlier today, and he wants us to join him in New York City to watch him wrestle at *The Final Stand*.

"Yeah? That'd be great," I said. "When will we leave?"

"We'll be flying out early Sunday morning. Just a quick trip. Dad will meet us there. He's making all the arrangements."

"But the show will end pretty late," I said. "What am I going to do about school the next day?"

I'm not sure why I said that. Any other time, I would have been glad for a chance to miss a day of school. But after what happened with Manny, I was feeling pretty good about myself. Also, for the first time since enrolling at Lanier, I had finally begun to feel like a part of the school.

She shrugged. "I guess you'll have to be out. I'll write your teachers a note, explaining the situation."

We don't usually attend live events to watch my father wrestle. I suppose it's like when parents take their kids to work to show them what they do for a living. It may be a treat to have their families there on occasion, but they don't want them there every day. It's the same with my father. For all of wrestling's spectacle and pomp, it's still just a job, and my father doesn't need us there getting in the way.

I suspected his invitation to join him had more to do with him trying to repair his and my mom's relationship.

"By the way, I've got something to show you." My mom rose from the couch. She opened the foyer closet and pulled out a black guitar case. "I bought it this morning. I want us to surprise Dad with it when he comes home tomorrow night."

"Wow!" I said. "Let me see it."

She handed it to me. I sat it down on the couch and opened the lid. Inside was a shiny, cream-colored, steel string Yamaha guitar.

"I hope he likes it," my mom said with uncertainty.

"Are you kidding? He's going to go absolutely nuts when he sees it."

I pulled the guitar out of its case and strummed it. It produced a dissonant sound.

"Maybe Dad can teach you how to play it," said my mom.

"Yeah, maybe," I replied. But I knew better. With the few days he spent at home, I doubted he would ever make time to teach me to play the guitar.

I placed the instrument back in its case. "Mom, I hope you don't mind, but I've invited a few friends over tonight to watch wrestling. Is that okay?"

She smiled. "Yes, of course, sweetheart. I'm glad to know you're making friends. Is everything else going okay at school?" Her voice sounded sincere, not accusatory.

"Sure. Oh, I almost forgot. Mrs. Petrosky wants to know if you've spoken to Dad about him visiting my school."

She sighed. "Jesse, I don't think he'll be able to do that."

I thought about Sara. That would be a perfect opportunity for her to meet him. "Dad says that he'll be taking a few weeks off after *The Final Stand*. Maybe he could make an appearance then," I told her.

"That'll be up to him and the company," she said doubtfully.

At about a quarter to eight, Wendell Cooley, Goose Guzman, Terrance Colby, and Ronnie Brisco showed up at my door.

"This is awesome!" exclaimed Wendell as they strolled into the den.

"Neato burrito!" cried Ronnie.

Like Mrs. Petrosky before them, they gawked at all the photographs hanging on the walls. I've been so used to living in the world of professional wrestling that it almost seems odd that people would be so awestruck by things I generally take for granted.

After they viewed the pictures in the den, I gave them a tour of my room. They were fascinated by my vast collection of wrestling action figures. Most of them were complimentary gifts from the toy manufacturing company that produces them.

"Hey, this one sort of looks like you, Wendy," teased Goose, holding up a toy of Jumbo Jefferson.

"And this one looks like your grandma," Wendell retorted, grabbing a toy of Butcher Murdock.

These guys are all right, I decided. Except for my friend, Eric, in St. Louis, it had been a long time since I'd had friends over to the house.

I turned on the TV. A few commercials later, the symphonic music of the ACW sounded and the colorful red, white, and blue words, AMERICAN CHAMPIONSHIP WRESTLING, flashed on the screen. Instantly, they burst in a fiery explosion. As the flames died out, the words were replaced with MONDAY NIGHT MAYHEM. The guys cheered with excitement, bouncing up and down on the couch.

The commentators, Simon Graham and Moose McGirk, wearing the company-issued blue blazers, white shirts, and red ties, welcomed the television audience to the show. They gave a rundown of the evening's matches, including an interview with the Angel of Death. The guys applauded loudly at the mention of my father's name.

My mom served us Cokes and a plate of store-bought raisin oatmeal cookies. Ronnie Brisco told my mom that he was allergic to raisins and asked if she had any other kinds of cookies. When she said no, he took a cookie and carefully plucked out the raisins before eating it.

The first match featured Jumbo Jefferson against Bruce the Bruiser Brannigan. Bruce Brannigan is a former ACW heavyweight champion. But he is forty-five years old and too many in-ring injuries have considerably slowed him down. The Bruiser, while still fairly skillful, is nevertheless used primarily as a jobber to push the younger guys.

"Get 'im," Bruiser!" shouted Goose, when Bruce Brannigan fought back after Jefferson's initial attack. Then, "One . . . two . . . " he counted along with the referee when Brannigan tried to pin Jefferson. Before the ref slapped the mat for a third time, however, Jefferson managed to kick out.

The two large men put on a great show, given their size. But most die-hard wrestling fans could've told you that Jumbo Jefferson was going to win the bout even before it began. Jefferson would be fighting Bronko Savage for the Iron Fist title on Sunday. The ACW was not about to have him lose a match on the last televised show before the pay-per-view event.

The guys didn't seem to know it, though. Since Bruce Brannigan played a face, they were rooting for him to beat the established heel, Jumbo Jefferson.

Finally, Jefferson got the upper hand, and after bouncing off the ropes, he plunged his 450-lb. body on his now helpless opponent. The referee counted to three and the match was over.

"Booo!" the guys shouted.

Watching wrestling through their eyes was fun. I hadn't enjoyed myself like this in quite a while. My mom passed by a couple of times to see if we needed anything. Despite the noise we were making, she didn't appear bothered by it. She was glad for me to have friends over.

Match after match, the guys made hilarious comments about the wrestlers. When Deuce Fargo, an aging, bald wrestler with a sagging chest was introduced, the guys chanted: "WHERE'S YOUR BRA? WHERE'S YOUR BRA?"

They broke into a chorus of barks when Bulldog Max Myers wrestled Kid Dynamo.

They jeered at the referees as they repeatedly failed to catch the heels, who were clearly cheating.

"What's the matter? Are you blind?" Wendell shouted at a referee who didn't see Gorgeous Gordon Gnash's feet hanging on the ropes for leverage as he illegally pinned Jumping Jackie Martin.

"They should get Bulldog Myers to serve as the ref's seeing-eye dog," joked Terrance.

I became a little nervous and embarrassed when Goose howled, "Aooohhh!" as Spirit made her way to the ring to face Andromeda, the women's champion, in a nontitle match. The rest of the guys joined him. Soon, our den sounded like a wolf convention. I worried that my mom would come in to investigate what all the howling was about and see Spirit on TV. Fortunately, the match didn't last very long. Andromeda pinned Spirit's shoulders with a quick roll up, ending the bout.

"Booo!" yelled Terrance. "I told you Spirit can't wrestle. Tell your dad to get her back as his valet."

I shot a quick glance toward my mom's bedroom door, hoping she hadn't heard him.

The show went to a commercial break. When it returned, the screen darkened and the Angel of Death's music began to play. The explosive pyrotechnic effects sent flames shooting into the air.

"Death! Death! Death! Death!" the guys shouted wildly.

My father, in his black attire and skeleton face make-up, appeared from a cloud of smoke and sauntered down the aisle.

I've got to admit that as many times as I've seen his ring entrance, I still get chills whenever I watch him. He stepped into the ring where Moose McGirk was waiting to interview him. As the music faded, the arena lights came back on.

"On Sunday night, at *The Final Stand*, you'll be defending your heavyweight title against Prince Romulus," said Moose McGirk. "Give us your impressions of the match."

My father rolled his eyeballs back into their sockets until only the whites of his eyes showed.

"From the depths of the darkest regions the Angel of Death shall appear, and Romulus shall rue that day. He will know the meaning of fear!" he bellowed in his deep, bass, robot-like voice.

My father delivers some of the cheesiest lines ever given in an interview. My mom called him a great poet, but Robert Frost, he definitely isn't.

"The ultimate price, O Prince, shall ye suffer, the Angel of Death doth command; prepare thee now to lose thy soul when we meet at The Final Stand! Aaagghh!" he roared, thrusting his scythe in the air.

The guys were completely "marking out" for my father's speech. A "mark" is a fan who believes that everything in professional wrestling is real. At least, they were accepting it as real for the moment. I hoped Sara was watching this.

Prince Romulus's music then blared from the sound system. The Prince, accompanied by Il Gran Mephisto, suddenly appeared at the top of the stage.

"Lose thy soul?" Mephisto cried into his handheld microphone, mocking my father. "Lose thy soul?" he repeated. "Listen to me, you putrid, rancid, walking carcass. Sunday night will be *your* final stand. When the Prince is finished with you, not only will he take away your title belt, he will send whatever's left of you back to the rotting, molding depths of the Netherworld. For good!" Prince Romulus smiled menacingly and nodded, rubbing his hands together.

With an air of confidence and arrogance, the two of them marched down the aisle. They climbed into the ring and faced my father.

"Tell us, Mephisto," said Moose McGirk, "How does your nephew plan to counter the sheer physical power of the Angel of Death?"

"Power?" Mephisto's voice thundered. "Power? Feel *my* power!" Il Gran Mephisto launched himself at my father, his hands extended, and hurled his flames at him. The Angel of Death ducked out of the way, but the fire caught Moose McGirk straight in the face.

"Whoa!" cried Terrance.

"*¡Hijo!*" yelled Goose.

"Awesome!" shouted Wendell.

"Eeeee!" shrieked Ronnie Brisco, covering his eyes.

"It's okay! He's not really burned," I told Ronnie, even as Moose McGirk fell to the canvas, grabbing his face, and bellowing in pain.

My father smacked Prince Romulus with a clothesline, flinging him over the ropes and onto the floor. He kicked Il Gran Mephisto in the stomach with his thick boot. Then he flipped him upside down and planted him on the mat with the Death Drop Pile Driver.

Simon Graham hysterically screamed, "Oh, my stars! Oh, my stars! Someone call the medics! The Moose has been shish kebabbed!"

The show cut to a commercial.

"How did he do that?" asked Wendell, aghast. "How does Il Gran Mephisto shoot fire from his fingers?"

I smiled. "If I tell you guys how he does it, do you swear you won't tell anyone?"

"Yeah," they promised eagerly.

"It has to be kept secret. It can't leave this room," I said in a hushed tone.

"I won't tell," said Goose, making the sign of the cross over his heart.

"Me either," said Terrance.

"Tell us," said Wendell, impatiently.

"All right," I said. "This is it." They huddled around me, as if they worried someone else might hear. "The reason Il Gran Mephisto can shoot flames with his hands is because . . ." I paused to let the suspense build.

"C'mon," cried Wendell. "Tell us."

"Okay," I said. "The reason he can shoot flames with his hands is because . . . Mephisto . . . eats a jarful of jalapeños and drinks a dozen bottles of Tabasco sauce every night before he climbs into the ring."

"Oh, brother," groaned Terrance.

"Come on, Jesse," begged Goose. "Tell us how he really does it."

"Don't you believe me?" I asked. "Why don't you try it and find out?"

"I think it's true," said Ronnie Brisco. "I had a cousin who tried something like that once, and — "

"Aw, shut up," said Wendell. He hit Ronnie over the head with a throw pillow. Ronnie picked it up and flung it back at him. Other pillows flew through the air. We laughed like crazy.

These guys *are* my friends, I thought. I felt a little ashamed that it took me so long to realize it.

CHAPTER FOURTEEN

The siren's blare made me jump. From the corner of my eye, I caught a glimpse of red, shiny, flashing lights. I hopped back on the curb, wondering if I had been caught jaywalking or something. The police squad car slowly pulled up to me.

"Jesse!" Sara called out as she rolled down the window from the passenger side.

"Hi." I approached the car, wondering what Sara was doing in it.

"Jesse, I'd like you to meet my dad, David Young." She turned to the police officer. "This is Jesse, Daddy, the wrestler's son."

The police officer, a slender man with sandy-colored hair and wire-framed sunglasses nodded. "Nice to meet you, Jesse. Sara's told me quite a bit about you."

"Nice to meet you too, sir." I reached across Sara and shook his hand.

"We watched your father on TV last night," he said. "I'd like to meet him sometime."

"I talked my parents into watching wrestling because the Angel of Death is our new neighbor," Sara explained when she saw the puzzled look on my face.

Her father didn't comment on the show. I couldn't tell if he liked it or not.

"Hop in. I'll give you a ride home," he offered.

As I slid into the backseat, Sara said, "Daddy's taking me to the pet salon to pick up our dog. I'm walking him home from there. It's not that far. Would you like to go with me?"

I shrugged indifferently. "Sure." I didn't want to give Officer Young any indication that I was interested in his daughter.

"Sara tells me your father once considered joining the San Antonio P.D.," said Officer Young.

"Yes, sir. But that was a long time ago."

He turned off the flashing lights and pulled away from the curb. "I'd like to invite him over to the station one of these days to give him a tour of the place," he said. "The guys would love to meet him. Some of the officers there are big wrestling fans."

"I'll tell him that, sir."

He still didn't give any hint of what he thought of the show.

A few minutes later he dropped us off at a place called The House of Wags.

Sara greeted the clerk, then produced a slip of paper.

"Haircut, shampoo, a cream rinse, and a fluff dry," the clerk read aloud from the receipt. "Nails clipped and ears cleaned. Gotcha. Back in a sec, hon."

She disappeared behind two double doors. Shortly, she returned with a tiny, white toy poodle.

"Here you go, hon. Clean as a whistle."

The dog instantly leaped into Sara's arms.

"This is Alaska," she said, cradling it.

"Hi, Alaska." I tried to pet the dog, but it growled at me.

"Alaska! That's rude," scolded Sara. "Jesse's my friend."

I don't think Alaska was convinced I was. She continued to growl until I backed away. Sara paid the clerk. She hooked a leash on Alaska's collar. Then we headed out the door.

"What did your dad think of the show last night?" I asked as we strolled down the sidewalk.

Sara tugged at the leash, pulling Alaska away from an empty beer can it was sniffing. She hesitated. Finally she said, "He really *does* want to meet your father."

"I'll buy that," I told her. "But what did he think about the show? Really."

Sara giggled nervously. "Well, to be truthful with you, Jesse, he told my mom that it was the worst acting he'd seen since they attended the Ed Wood Film Festival."

"Who's Ed Wood?" I asked.

Sara shrugged. "I don't know, but my mom seemed to understand what he was talking about, because she laughed and nodded."

"Oh, well. They're entitled to their opinions," I said, dismissing the criticism. "So why does he want to meet my father?"

"Actually, my parents want to meet your father *and* your mother. After all, they did buy the Bennetts' house. They're curious about who Mr. and Mrs. Bennett sold the house to. You know, they're being . . . " Sara pointed at her nose. She frowned, then whispered, "Nosy. Also, my dad knows your father is a celebrity. I think he wants to be able to tell his friends he knows the Angel of Death."

"But he doesn't even like wrestling."

"I'm not so sure he doesn't," said Sara. "After your dad's interview, he sent me upstairs to get ready for bed. But he kept the TV tuned to channel 36, and he and my mom watched the rest of the show."

We turned the corner and cut through the park. Alaska pranced to a nearby tree, sniffed it, and did her business.

From a short distance away, I spotted a familiar figure. The *paletero* was stationed under a large pecan tree. It was the same old man from whom Sara had bought the ice creams the other day. He was surrounded by a mob of little kids.

"Want an ice cream?" I offered. "My treat."

"Sure," said Sara.

We made our way to the *paletero*. "*Dos de sandía, por favor*," I said confidently. I hoped Sara would be impressed with my Spanish. The old man produced two watermelon-flavored ice creams from inside his cart.

After I paid him, Sara and I sat on the swings and ate our ice creams. She tossed her wrapper on the ground for Alaska to lick. The dog appeared to like watermelon-flavored ice cream as much as I did.

"Are you sure they don't have *paleteros* in St. Louis?" Sara queried. "Because if they don't, they're missing a piece of heaven." She bit the tip of her ice cream and slowly savored it.

"I never said St. Louis didn't have any *paleteros*. I just never saw one," I told her. "But then, we didn't live there that long, anyway."

"Oh? Where did you live before?"

I rolled my eyes. "A better question is, where haven't I lived."

Sara gave me a puzzled look. "What do you mean?"

"What I mean is, we've lived in just about every city in the United States."

I tossed my ice cream wrapper next to Alaska. The dog eyed me suspiciously for a moment before deciding that it was safe to lick it.

"Okay, I'm exaggerating, but there have been times when I've felt like it."

Sara smiled. "All right, let's start from the beginning. Where were you born?"

"Actually, I was born in Dallas, but we moved from there when I was about six months old. My father had just begun his wrestling career, and the company he wrestled for, a small outfit called Southwest Wrestling Association, soon folded. He and some of the wrestlers from the SWA joined another independent wrestling organization in Phoenix called National Pro Wrestling. But that one shut down, too. After that, he wrestled for the Universal Wrestling League. That one went under in less than two years, and my father had to find another job."

Sara furrowed her brows. "How could these organizations go out of business? I would think that with all the people who love wrestling, they'd be booming."

"You'd think so," I agreed. "But the truth is, most fans only follow the major wrestling leagues like the ACW. The smaller companies can't begin to compete with them, especially if they don't have a TV contract. Anyway, my father bounced around from company to company, getting beaten and battered night after night for next to no money. Pay in the independent circuit is minimal, to say the least. Sometimes my mom worked as a substitute teacher to help ends meet."

"Life's been rough, huh?" said Sara.

"Yeah, a little. Mostly, it's all the moving. Do you know I've been at ten different schools since kindergarten?"

I hopped off the swing and stooped to pick up the ice cream wrappers from the ground. Alaska snarled and barked at me when I tried to take hers.

"I'll get that one," said Sara. "Shame on you, Alaska. Quit being so mean to Jesse." The dog shied away, her head hung low.

"So, how long do you plan to stay in San Antonio?" she asked.

A butterfly raced through my insides. I hoped she was asking because she cared about whether I stayed or left.

"For good, I hope. Both my parents were born here, and they've always wanted to return to San Antonio." I paused, then added, "I'm not sure it matters, anyway."

"What do you mean?"

I sighed. "Sara, my father is on the road . . . a lot! Last year, he was out of town over three hundred days. We hardly ever see him. He and my mom argue about it all the time. She wants him to leave the wrestling business."

"He's not going to, is he?" Sara asked, sounding worried.

I shrugged. "He's talked about it, but he enjoys it too much. I doubt he'll ever quit. Not soon, anyway."

Sara nodded. "Sounds like my father. He works all kinds of crazy hours, too, plus second jobs. We hardly ever see him, either. He's been eligible to retire for a while, but he won't. He really likes being a police officer. My mom's come to terms with that, so she tries not to complain about it."

"How about you?" I asked. "How do *you* feel about it?"

"I don't think about it, really. I mean, he's been a police officer all my life. I can't imagine him doing anything else."

I wondered whether I was being selfish, wishing my father wouldn't be gone so much if his job required it. Was I wrong to feel jealous when he spent time with other kids? After all, it *is* part of his job. I had to agree with Sara; I couldn't imagine my father ever being anything other than the Angel of Death.

I thought about that as I headed home after seeing Sara off at her house.

CHAPTER FIFTEEN

At around nine o'clock on Sunday morning, my father met us at J.F.K. International Airport. Since there is a time difference between New York and San Antonio, my watch read an hour earlier. I was still pretty tired. I'd tried to sleep on the plane, but I was too excited about the trip and watching my father wrestle live at *The Final Stand*.

The last pay-per-view event I attended was *Retribution* when it was held in Atlanta, Georgia. The only reason I got to go then was because we were living in Atlanta at the time.

My father had been in New York since Friday. He, along with many of the ACW superstars, had participated in autograph signing sessions at various locations in and around the New York area to hype the show.

"I've got to be at Madison Square Garden by one o'clock," my father informed us.

From the airport he took us out to eat breakfast at a small, crowded café called The Rooster's Crow. No one recognized my father, or if they did, they didn't bother him.

Perhaps in New York, people are more accustomed to seeing celebrities in public and it isn't a big deal to them.

The waiter was prompt, but curt. He didn't smile or make small talk. He simply took our order and brought out our food. Strangely, his aloof attitude was a welcomed change.

As we ate, my father went over the details of his match with us. The information was mainly for my benefit. He didn't want me to worry about him.

I had guessed correctly. Il Gran Mephisto *was* going to "burn" my father's face during his bout with Prince Romulus. The Prince would get disqualified, so my father would keep his title. But the burning episode would explain why the Angel of Death wouldn't be seen on television for the next four weeks.

One of the reasons my father stopped taking me to watch him wrestle was because, when I was younger, I used to get so emotional whenever his opponents started beating him up.

There was the time, for example, when I almost jumped into the ring to save my father. I must've been about five. He was still wrestling as the Annihilator. His opponent that night was a wrestler called Cowboy Bobby Travis. Cowboy Bobby was the face in the match, and the whole arena was rooting for him to trounce the Annihilator. It didn't matter to me that my father was playing a heel. He was still my father. Cowboy Bobby knocked him down in the corner of the ring and started stomping him with his big cowboy boots, much to the delight of the crowd. Even though I knew wrestling was scripted, watching my father get beaten up was too much to bear. I completely forgot that he really wasn't getting hurt. With tears streaming down my face, I yelled at the top of my lungs for Cowboy Bobby to stop. Finally, I sprang from my seat and raced to the ring.

"Leave my daddy alone, you big bully!" I shouted. I was halfway inside the ring before a security guard seized me by my legs.

My mom, who had been talking to Aunt Gracie during the match, hadn't noticed that I had left my chair. The audience began booing when the security guard grabbed me.

They thought it was funny watching a little kid trying to climb into the ring to rescue the Annihilator.

The boos grew louder. Finally, my mom turned to see what was happening. To her horror, she saw me struggling in the security guard's arms. She flew down to ringside. The security guard, however, didn't want to release me. He was concerned that I might jump back into the ring. My mom started hollering at him as she tried to pry me from his arms. The crowd, now ignoring the match, urged her on, loudly cheering, laughing, and applauding.

Meanwhile, my father was no longer selling Cowboy Bobby's kicks. Through his mask, his eyes bulged out like Ping-Pong balls. His mouth hung open as he gawked at the growing chaos. Breaking out of character, he rose to his feet. He shoved Cowboy Bobby Travis out of the way and stormed up to us. He ordered the security guard to escort my mom and me to the back.

Luckily for his career, the incident occurred at a house show, and it was never aired.

When we were through eating, my father drove us around and gave us a quick tour of New York City. We walked for a while around Times Square, visiting some of the shops. We stopped briefly at the hotel where my father was staying to drop off our things. After that we headed to the arena.

CHAPTER SIXTEEN

Madison Square Garden was energetically charged with bustling crew members. Dressed in red jumpsuits that sported the ACW logo, they resembled a colony of ants. The crew was busily transforming the building into the wrestling extravaganza that would be presented later that evening. Some were assembling the ring, piece by piece, like a jigsaw puzzle, at center stage. Others, on towering scaffolds, hung various types of special effects lights. A pyrotechnics crew set up the explosives that would be detonated for the wrestlers' entrances. The sound manager ordered a test run of the equipment. Television cameras were strategically stationed throughout the arena.

After my father checked in, we strolled around the corridors.

Backstage, the place looked like a monster's reunion. Gargantuan, muscled wrestlers gathered in groups, chatting. It had been so long since I'd been to a live event that I'd almost forgotten how big the wrestlers are in person. They say TV adds pounds, giving the illusion that people on screen are heavier than they really are. Staring at Jumbo Jefferson's humongous frame, I realized that TV offered no clue as to how enormous he really is.

"How's it going, Mark?" A wrestler unfamiliar to me approached my father and shook his hand. "All set for tonight?"

It took me a moment to recognize Prince Romulus. Wearing jeans and a golf shirt instead of his colorful ring garb, he looked like plain old Scott Blanchard from Detroit.

"Hi, Scotty. I'd like you to meet my family," my father said.

"A pleasure to meet you, Molly. You too, Jesse. Mark talks about you all the time." There was no trace in his voice of the Italian accent he uses on television.

"Has Mephisto arrived?" asked my father.

"Yeah, I spoke to him a little while ago. He's in the dressing room practicing his flame trick."

"You be careful with my husband, Scott," cautioned my mom. "I wouldn't want anything to ruin this beautiful face." She squeezed my father's cheeks tightly and kissed him.

"Don't worry, Mrs. Baron," said the Prince. "We'll take good care of him. Anyway, Mark would make for terrible barbecue."

After my father introduced us to some more wrestlers, we found his dressing room. His Angel of Death costume was neatly hung in a plastic bag, courtesy of Shirley Washington, the woman in charge of maintaining the wrestlers' outfits.

He dropped off his bags, and we headed for the lunch area.

Long tables and chairs had been set up in a wide, open space. Wrestlers, staff members, and the work crew stood in double lines and waited to serve themselves at the buffet table—a feast of fish, chicken, salad, green beans, mashed potatoes, and fruit.

Carlos "El Azteca Dorado" Montoya and his wife, Melba, joined us for lunch. Prince Romulus and Il Gran

Mephisto sat across from us. It was odd to think that in a few short hours, my father and these two men would be battling each other in the ring.

While we ate, Cassandra "Spirit" Richardson stopped by our table.

She greeted my mom with a warm smile and a hug. "Hello, Molly, it's so good to see you. I'm glad you could make it."

"Yes, it's good to see you, too," my mom said with no emotion in her voice. She didn't return the smile and barely made eye contact.

Spirit must have sensed the hostility. She stepped back and said, "See you around." She left to find a seat at another table, although there was plenty of room at ours.

When we had finished eating, my mom met up with some of the other wives and girlfriends. After a bit of socializing, they decided to leave Madison Square Garden to do some shopping.

I stayed behind to hang out with my father. It was great to be able to spend time with him, something I rarely had a chance to do. We didn't talk a whole lot, since he was visiting with his friends. But I didn't mind, really. I loved listening to them swap stories.

"Herman," said Red Lassiter, "Tell the boys about the time we got pulled over by the cops in Arkansas."

Herman "Kronos" Berkowitz had smeared a greasy ointment over the welts on his face. His skin now glistened with an orange-red tone.

"Aw, most of da guys already hoid dat story."

"Not everyone. I'll bet Carlos Montoya hasn't heard it. Have you, Carlos?"

"No, what happened?"

"You tell it, Red," said Kronos. "You tell it better den I do."

Red Lassiter jumped up on one of the packing crates and sat down. "You see, Herman and I had just finished a show in Little Rock. Even though we had already showered and changed, Herman insisted on putting his mask back on. He wanted to wear it until we drove away from the arena. You know, for the fans who were hanging around after the matches to catch a final glimpse of us. Well, we had just pulled out and were heading to the highway when, from my rearview mirror, I caught sight of flashing red lights. Apparently a taillight from our rental was out or something." Red Lassiter chuckled. He hopped off the crate and paced around, gesturing with his hands as he told the story. "Anyway, one of the cops approached the car. The second he spotted Herman in his Kronos mask, he pulled out his gun and ordered us out. The other cop, watching his partner, bolted out of the squad car wielding a shotgun. They made us lie down on the asphalt street, face down. We tried to tell them we were wrestlers, but they wouldn't listen." His chuckling escalated into a hearty laugh.

"Yeah, I tried to remove da mask, but dey made me keep my hands behind my back," Kronos said, joining in the laughter.

"They called in our driver's license numbers," said Red. "We checked out okay, but that still didn't explain why Herman was wearing a mask. The cops then ordered him to remove it."

"Dat's what I'd been trying to do da whole time," Kronos broke in.

"Finally, we convinced them we were wrestlers, and they let us go," said Red.

"Tank god I won't hafta wear dat rag on my face after tonight," said Kronos.

At around three o'clock, Harold Becker, the head writer for ACW, met with my father, Prince Romulus, Il Gran Mephisto, and Rocky Davis, the referee who would be officiating their match, in one of the corridors.

"I want to go over the finish with you one more time," Mr. Becker told them as he scanned his notes on his clipboard. "When Rocky gives you the signal, Angel, you'll use an Irish Whip to send the Prince against the ropes. Prince, you'll bounce back, and he'll hit you with a clothesline. As soon as you fall to the mat, Angel will climb the turnbuckles and jump off with an elbow drop. Except that at the last second, Prince, you'll move out of the way, and Angel will miss his target. At this point, Angel, you'll roll out of the ring and land on the floor, holding your elbow in pain. Mephisto, this is where you come in. While the Prince distracts Rocky, you'll sneak up on Angel and shoot your flames, burning his face. Rocky, you'll catch him in the act and call for the bell. The match ends in a disqualification. No title change. At that point, while Angel is on the floor in agony, the both of you will attack him. Rocky will call for backup to separate you. After you're sent to the back, the paramedics will rush out with a gurney. They'll wheel Angel away to a waiting ambulance. The camera crew will capture the whole thing on film, and everyone goes home happy."

Harold Becker and his team of writers generally map out the finish to each match. Sometimes the wrestlers will offer their input, but ultimately, Frank Collins makes the final decision on the direction of each bout.

The referees wear hidden earpieces. They receive their instructions from one of the ACW officials backstage that oversees the matches. When the time comes to end a match, the official speaks to the referee through his earpiece. The ref then gives the signal to the wrestlers, saying something like, "Let's go home." After that, they follow the script and end the match.

"Irish Whip, clothesline, missed elbow drop, flames, end of match," Harold Becker repeated. "Any questions?"

The four men shook their heads.

"All right, good luck to all of you. Let's give the fans a good show." Mr. Becker left to visit some of the other wrestlers. Rocky Davis accompanied him.

I followed my father as he, Prince Romulus, and Il Gran Mephisto made their way to the ring, which stood in the middle of the cavernous arena, to go over some of their moves. Except for a few crew members who were still setting up, the place was empty. Mephisto and I sat down at ringside while my father and the Prince entered the ring.

Although this was the first time they would meet in a televised match, my father and the Prince had wrestled each other in house shows on numerous occasions, so they were familiar with each other's styles.

Methodically, they practiced each hold and move — body slams, arm bars, ankle locks, drop kicks, and suplexes, as well as my father's finishing maneuver, the Death Drop Pile Driver, and Prince Romulus's submission hold, the Procrustes Stretch.

Only the endings of the matches are scripted. The wrestlers are free to call their moves as they see fit. Throughout their match, they talk to each other, calling their spots. For instance, while my father has Prince Romulus wrapped in a headlock and the Prince is wailing in pain, my father might whisper something to him like, "Irish Whip, body press, drop kick." The Prince then knows to throw my father against the ropes, and as the ropes fling him back, the Prince will fly up and sail his body against my father's, knocking him down to the canvas. When my father stands up, the Prince then jumps up in the air, and with both feet, he'll kick him, sending him back down to the mat. At that point, the Prince may try to pin him. My father will kick out, of course. The Prince then grabs my father in a headlock of his own, where they'll have an opportunity to call the next spot. Because of the loud, raucous crowds, no one hears what the men are saying to one another.

After about twenty minutes, my father and the Prince were done. Il Gran Mephisto handed them towels to wipe off the perspiration they'd worked up.

"About those flames, Mephisto," my father said, warily, "are you absolutely positive they don't burn?"

At breakfast this morning, my father had expressed his concern about having fire thrown in his face, even though he'd seen Il Gran Mephisto perform the stunt countless times.

"Don't worry, Mark, it's perfectly safe," Mephisto assured him. "Watch." He flung his arms out and launched a yellow-orange fireball, as if by magic, from his hands.

"Aaah!" yelled my father. He jumped back, stumbled on the ring steps, and fell.

I gasped and ran to see if his face was burned. Il Gran Mephisto and the Prince howled with laughter.

"I told you it was safe, Mark," said Mephisto as he reached out to pull him up.

My father gave an embarrassed chuckle as he stood. He rubbed his cheeks to check for any signs of pain. I was relieved to see that he was all right. That fireball looked frighteningly dangerous.

"Man, that scared the devil out of me, Mephisto," said my father. "Why didn't you warn me you were going to do that?"

"That's what it'll look like tonight, Mark," replied Il Gran Mephisto. "It'll happen that fast. Be ready for it."

It would be something to watch, I thought. But no matter what Mephisto told my father, I knew the flame-shooting trick wasn't as safe as he claimed. Even with years of practice doing that stunt, there was always a chance that something could go wrong. I just hoped that tonight wasn't the night when it would happen.

My father and I returned to his dressing room. He took a quick shower. Then he dressed in his black leather Angel of Death outfit.

"Dad, you look like Zorro," I told him. "All you need is the mask."

"I think you're right, champ," he said, gazing at himself in the mirror on the dressing table. "Maybe after the Angel of Death gimmick plays itself out, I'll become Zorro for a while." He picked up his scythe and swung it in the air.

"Wherever there is injustice, wherever wrong and inequality reign, the tyrants shall fall by the edge of the sword, when Zorro shall ride again!"

As he whipped his scythe to form a Z in the air, he accidentally struck and smashed the dressing table mirror.

"Dad!"

He dropped his scythe, sending it clanging to the floor. "Uh-oh. I guess I'd better stick to being the Angel of Death," he said, blushing. "Let's get out of here."

"But what about the mirror?" I asked, aghast. "Won't you get in trouble for breaking it?"

He stared at the shattered glass and shrugged. "Only if you believe in the superstition of having seven years of bad luck." He smiled and tousled my hair. "Besides, lots worse damage has been done to dressing rooms than this. Come on, let's see if we can find Connie."

Connie Herrera heads the makeup department for the ACW. Some wrestlers require only a touch of make-up to bring out the color of their faces or to remove the shine that results from perspiration. One of Connie's assistants does that job. With my father, however, with his intricately detailed skeleton face design, the task is much more complicated, and Connie handles that responsibility herself. A partitioned area in one of the corridors made up the makeup room.

While Connie worked on my father, I sat down and read through a copy of *American Championship Wrestling Magazine*, the program that would be sold later at one of several souvenir stands. Most of the magazine was actually a catalog where fans could order ACW merchandise, but it also contained articles about some of the wrestlers, as well as a list of tonight's matches.

I was reading an article about Tashira Nagasaki, a Japanese wrestler who would be facing El Azteca Dorado on tonight's card, when I heard Connie say, "All done, Mark. You are one handsome creature, if I do say so myself."

I glanced up from my magazine and stared at my father. My mouth fell open. He rose slowly from his chair and walked toward me. His immense presence cast a deep shadow, blocking out the light.

"Aaagghh!" he roared, thrusting his arms in the air. His eyeballs rolled back until only the whites were visible.

"D–Dad?"

"Echoes of vengeance cry out in the night; the Angel of Death hath emerged. To vanquish thee, Prince, and restore what is right, thine existence shall forever be purged! Aaagghh!"

My insides bubbled with both jitters and joy. It had been a long time since I'd seen him in full costume up close. He was an amazing sight.

Maybe I didn't have the perfect father. Maybe things at home weren't as ideal as I wished they could be. But at that moment, I felt a tremendous sense of pride. This was my father . . . the Angel of Death.

CHAPTER SEVENTEEN

Shortly after we left Connie's makeup area, my father cut a promo for television that would air later in the show, just prior to his match. Penelope Precious conducted the interview. Before my father spoke, Penelope Precious, an occasional on-the-air personality, who in reality is Frank Collins's wife, Terri, explained to the viewing audience that she was substituting for Moose McGirk, the regular interviewer, while he recovered from the serious burns he had suffered at the hands of Il Gran Mephisto.

"On behalf of everyone here at ACW, I want to take this moment to wish Moose McGirk a speedy recovery from the horrendous and despicable attack he suffered last Monday night," she said somberly before the camera. "Get well soon, Moose. Our thoughts are with you." Penelope Precious's voice cracked, and she dabbed her eyes with a tissue.

I had to do everything I could to keep from laughing. Moose McGirk was standing a few feet away, talking with Harold Becker. The Moose appeared to be in perfect health. There were no burn marks anywhere on his face.

Like my father, the Moose had requested, and had been granted, some time off. Penelope Precious would fill in as Simon Graham's commentating partner until the Moose returned.

My father's interview was his basic shtick, bad poetry and all. In his gravelly, monotone voice, he promised to send the Prince's soul to *the depths of the Netherworld.*

When he was through, he returned to his dressing room to do some stretching exercises. I strolled around the back, hoping to run into my mom. I figured she'd be returning any moment.

"Gimme back my comic book!" I heard Kronos yell as I neared the "ready room." The door was open so I peeked in.

"You don't know how to read anyway," retorted Ice Man Jacob Sloane. He was holding a Batman comic in the air, away from Kronos's reach. "You can have it back when I'm through with it."

"Give Herman back his comic book," Karl Nelson, a.k.a. the Black Mamba, ordered. He reached out, grabbed Sloane's arm, and twisted it into a wrist lock. In the ring, wrist locks are applied without much force. Wrestlers are careful not to hurt each other. But this wasn't a staged fight; it was a shoot, a real one.

"Aaahh! Let go of my arm!" screamed Jacob Sloane.

"Give him back his comic book and I will," Black Mamba replied with eerie calmness. He had a four-inch height and seventy-pound weight advantage over Jacob Sloane.

Sloane released the comic book and let it drop to the floor.

"Uh-uh. Pick it up and hand it to him," Mamba ordered, still gripping the Ice Man's wrist.

Reluctantly, Sloane stooped down, retrieved the comic book, and handed it back to Kronos.

"Now let's try to act like gentlemen back here, okay?" said Mamba.

Sloane silently slithered out of the ready room, massaging his wrist.

Evidently, Carlos Montoya wasn't the only one who had grown tired of the Ice Man's antics.

"Tanks, Karl," said Kronos, "but I coulda handled that joik myself."

"I know, but believe me, Herman, the pleasure was all mine," Mamba said with a smile.

Top stars like my father are often provided with an individual dressing room. But most of the wrestlers share a large locker room that is commonly referred to as the "ready room."

The wrestlers in the ready room had already changed into their wrestling attire, although Kronos hadn't slipped on his mask. He would probably wait until right before his match to do so. But El Azteca Dorado, the Black Mamba, and the Blue Dragon already had theirs on.

I walked around the ready room and greeted the wrestlers. Most were pretty friendly and said hello, but a few, like Lars Price, a.k.a. Dr. Inferno, merely grunted without looking up at me.

Sean LaRue of the Midnight Raiders sat at a table playing chess with Kid Dynamo. Gorgeous Gordon Gnash listened to music through his headphones that were plugged into his iPod. Bruce the Bruiser Brannigan quietly read his Bible. And Jason Cage, Red Lassiter, and Bulldog Max Myers played a video game on one of the TV monitors. Kronos settled himself back in his chair with his stack of comic books.

"Hey, kid, come here," a voice called out. I turned around. "Give this to your old man. I think he's gonna need it."

Demented Devlin Dredd handed me my father's scythe.

What was he doing with it? I wondered.

Devlin Dredd apparently read the baffled expression on my face. "I needed something to sharpen my pencil with."

I glanced down and spotted a crossword puzzle on his lap.

"By the way, kid, you know a five-letter word for *enclosure*?" he asked.

I shook my head.

Sean LaRue looked up from his chess game. "How about *pound*? Which is what Angel's gonna do to you when he finds out you took his scythe."

Dredd, ignoring LaRue's warning, jotted down the answer on his puzzle. "From the looks of Angel's dressing room mirror, it looks like he's already done a bit of pounding. There was glass everywhere when I went in there." He gave me a mischievous smile. "You know anything about that, kid?"

"Um, you'll have to ask my father about that."

Carefully holding the scythe upright to avoid striking anything or anyone with it, I retreated to my father's dressing room.

He was on the floor doing pushups when I entered. The glass on the dressing table had been cleared off. He looked up. "What are you doing with that?"

"Devlin Dredd had it, Dad," I told him. "He told me to bring it back to you." I hoped he didn't think that I'd taken it.

He rose to his feet and took the scythe. "What was Dredd doing with it?" My father rolled it in his hands and examined it.

"He used it to sharpen his pencil," I said. "He was working a crossword puzzle, and his pencil point broke, so I guess . . . "

"To sharpen his pencil?" My father shook his head. "Go back and tell Devlin Dredd that being demented isn't just a gimmick he uses in the ring. Tell him . . . "

Suddenly the national anthem blared from inside the auditorium.

"Never mind. The show's starting." He leaned his scythe against a wall. "Go in and watch it."

"But Mom's not back yet."

"Don't worry about her. I'll have her meet you as soon as she comes in."

AMERICAN CHAMPIONSHIP WRESTLING
PRESENTS
THE FINAL STAND

SUNDAY NIGHT • MADISON SQUARE GARDEN • NEW YORK

ACW HEAVYWEIGHT TITLE

THE ANGEL OF DEATH **VS.** **PRINCE ROMULUS**

(CHAMPION) **(CHALLENGER)**

MASK VS. MASK

KRONOS **VS.** **BLACK MAMBA**

IRON FIST TITLE

BRONKO SAVAGE **VS.** **JUMBO JEFFERSON**

(CHAMPION) **(CHALLENGER)**

STEEL CAGE MATCH

ICE MAN JACOB SLOANE VS. **BUTCHER MURDOCK**

ACW TAG-TEAM TITLES

JASON CAGE **KID DYNAMO**

(CHAMPION) **(CHALLENGER)**

& **VS.** **&**

SEAN LARUE **RED LASSITER**

(CHAMPION)

ACW WOMEN'S TITLE

ANDROMEDA **VS.** **LIBBA T. BELLE**

(CHAMPION) **(CHALLENGER)**

EAST MEETS WEST

TASHIRA NAGASAKI **VS.** **EL AZTECA DORADO**

Plus three other great matches

CHAPTER EIGHTEEN

Every seat in Madison Square Garden was sold out. Luckily my father had reserved a couple of them on the third row for my mom and me.

Boisterous and rowdy fans decorated the auditorium with handmade signs and banners they'd brought from home to show their enthusiasm and support for their favorite wrestlers, as well as to show their displeasure for those they hated.

The cameras panned the room for crowd shots. I thought about Wendell and the guys sitting in his living room watching *The Final Stand*. Every time the cameras were pointed in my direction, I jumped up and down and waved my arms like a maniac, hoping they would see me on TV.

All of a sudden, the heavy metal music for the Midnight Raiders blasted through the speakers. Multi-colored laser lights flashed across the auditorium. Sean LaRue and Jason Cage, the ACW tag-team champions, appeared at the top of the stage. They were dressed in similar navy blue tights with matching navy blue boots. They wore black vests speckled with tiny white stars. MIDNIGHT RAIDERS was emblazoned on the back of their vests in shiny gold letters.

They raced down the entrance ramp, slapping hands with the fans as they made their way to the ring.

Seconds later, their challengers, Red Lassiter and Kid Dynamo, followed them. After the introductions for the tag-team title match, the bout was underway.

Although I tune in to watch wrestling almost every Monday night, there is nothing like seeing it live. The match was fast-paced, with lots of moves, countermoves, and near pins. Finally, after about twelve minutes, Jason Cage pinned Kid Dynamo with the Raider Roll while their partners fought outside the ring. It was a terrific opening match, and the fans demonstrated their appreciation by giving the wrestlers a standing ovation.

The second match featured El Azteca Dorado against Tashira Nagasaki. The article in the *American Championship Wrestling Magazine* dubbed it the "East Meets West" match. It was an exciting bout that, like the first one, featured almost nonstop action. In the end, though, Nagasaki made El Azteca Dorado tap out when he clamped a Cross Face Chicken Wing on him.

Carlos Montoya had known beforehand that he would job to Tashira Nagasaki, but he didn't mind. In wrestling, it's not a matter of winning or losing a match as much as it is about entertaining the fans. And the match *was* entertaining. Carlos Montoya's *lucha libre* style of wrestling blended perfectly with Tashira Nagasaki's martial arts moves. Their match showcased their impressive acrobatic abilities.

My mom finally arrived during the middle of the match between Jumbo Jefferson and Bronko Savage.

"Where were you?" I asked. "I was starting to get worried."

I didn't tell her, but what really worried me was what my father might have thought of her leaving after he'd made all these plans to have us be here with him.

"Sorry, sweetheart," she said, panting for breath. "We lost track of time and then we got lost. Anyway, I'm here. Did I miss much?"

I gave her a brief rundown of what had happened so far.

Bronko Savage started strong, pummeling Jefferson with some vicious right hands. But Jumbo Jefferson soon recovered. Even though the match was billed as a fight for the Iron Fist title, he mostly used his incredibly large body to his advantage rather than his fists. He tossed Bronko Savage against the corner. Jefferson followed that up with a fierce Avalanche, sending Savage crumbling down to the mat. Then, with a running start, he flew up and crashed down on him with the Jumbo Splash. One, two, three, and Jumbo Jefferson was declared the new Iron Fist champion.

The next bout was the Mask vs. Mask match between Kronos and Black Mamba. Because of their enormous sizes, this match, like the one before, had none of the aerial maneuvers that the first two bouts offered. Mostly they pounded and kicked each other. The end of the match came when Mamba managed to break out of a Full Nelson, tagging Kronos on the jaw with an elbow smash. Then he slammed his head against the turnbuckles. With Kronos now dazed, Mamba lifted him and suplexed him solidly onto the mat. He dragged Kronos back to his feet with a side headlock. Then, to advertise what he was about to do next, Mamba raised his right arm in the air. His hand was balled in a fist, and his thumb stuck out like a hitchhiker's. It was wrapped with shiny gold tape. The fans shrieked with excitement. Mamba jammed his thumb in Kronos's throat. It was his famous "Mamba Stinger." Kronos struggled to break out of the hold, kicking and flaying his arms, but after a few seconds, his legs started to buckle. His body slumped down to the canvas. Mamba, his thumb still firmly planted in Kronos's neck, then climbed on top of him. The referee counted to three, punctuating each number with a loud hand slap to the mat.

"THE WINNER OF THE MASK VS. MASK MATCH," Dan Greenberg screamed into the microphone, "BLAAACK MAMBAAA!"

The crowd cheered wildly.

Black Mamba climbed the corner ropes and raised his arms in triumph while the thoroughly entertained fans chanted: "*Mamba! Mamba! Mamba!*" He leaped off and ran to the opposite corner and did the same thing. Making sure not to leave anyone out, Mamba climbed up the other two corners, letting the fans know how much he valued their support.

After the noise subsided, Mamba snatched the microphone away from Dan Greenberg. He aimed a finger, pistol-like, at his prostrate opponent. "Take off your mask, Kronos!" he commanded. Kronos slowly staggered to his feet. He stared at Mamba in horror. Then he turned to the audience and comically shook his head.

"Your mask!" Mamba roared. "Take it off!" He pantomimed yanking off his own mask.

"No! No!" bawled Kronos. He pressed his mask tightly against his face and pleaded his case with the fans.

The crowd was having none of it. "Take it off!" they yelled. "Take it off!"

What an act, I thought. Nothing would please Kronos more than to strip off his mask right then and there, but he was acting as if it was the worst possible thing that could happen to him. He was Br'er Rabbit begging Br'er Fox not to throw him into the briar patch.

Finally, Frank Collins appeared at the top of the stage holding a microphone of his own.

"Kronos," he called, "I'm ordering you to take your mask off right now! That was the stipulation you agreed to when you signed the contract to this match. Take it off or you will be facing an indefinite suspension."

The announcement thrilled the crowd. "Take it off! Take it off! Take it off!"

Kronos, left with no other alternative, began to undo the laces on his mask. He paused momentarily and turned to Frank Collins. He fell to his knees and clasped his hands as if in prayer. But Mr. Collins, unmoved by Kronos's actions, yelled into his microphone, "Come on, Kronos! Take it off!"

At last, Kronos peeled off his red and white mask. The fans laughed and jeered at him. Black Mamba raised his arms triumphantly once again as his theme music hit.

His face now bare, Kronos dejectedly climbed out of the ring and walked through a gauntlet of unceasing taunts and insults. But I knew that inside he was smiling, relieved that finally he would no longer have to wrestle with a mask suffocating his face.

Next on the card was the Women's Title match with Andromeda successfully defending her belt against a former women's champ, Libba T. Belle.

Gorgeous Gordon Gnash lost by disqualification to Dr. Inferno when he grabbed his atomizer from the ringside announcer's table and sprayed perfume into Inferno's eyes.

Demented Devlin Dredd defeated Bruce the Bruiser Brannigan with a Brainbuster, and the Blue Dragon got a win over Bulldog Max Myers when he knocked him out with a Super Kick.

It had been an incredible show so far. I knew Wendell and the guys were enjoying every minute of it. I hoped Sara was watching, too. But I knew it was unlikely. If her parents didn't allow her to watch wrestling when it was free on TV, they certainly weren't about to shell out the bucks to order the pay-per-view. I'd tell her all about it when I got back to school.

The steel cage, which had been suspended above the arena all night, now slowly descended until it encircled the ring for the next match.

Butcher Murdock was introduced first. He snarled and growled at the fans as he paraded past them. The fans booed him in return. Murdock entered the ring through a small door on the side of the cage.

By contrast, as he marched down the aisle, Ice Man Jacob Sloane, overwhelmingly the fan favorite, was greeted with unrestrained cheers and applause. A teenage girl held up a sign that read: MARRY ME, ICE MAN!

Pro wrestling has a way of influencing the fans to accept what it wants them to believe. Butcher Murdock, who outside of the ring is one of the nicest men I've ever met, plays a heel. So most fans automatically hate him. On the other hand, the fans idolize Jacob Sloane because he portrays a good guy, a face. But I wonder how the fans, particularly the girl with the MARRY ME, ICE MAN sign would feel if they knew what a jerk he was in real life.

The Steel Cage match lived up to its hype. It was a vicious, bloody battle with both men blading heavily. I'm sure Manny, if he was watching, was marking out for it, big time. The fans at Madison Square Garden certainly were.

"Jesse, I'm going to step out into the lobby for a little bit," my mom said, looking queasy. I'd have thought that after seeing my father blade over the years, she'd have gotten used to it. Apparently she hadn't.

"Okay, but Dad's match is coming up next," I reminded her.

After a grueling twenty minutes, Ice Man Jacob Sloane finally won the match, leaving Butcher Murdock laying unconscious in the ring, bleeding profusely.

As battered as both men looked, I knew they were okay. They hadn't really beaten each other as badly as they would like the fans to think. The punches the wrestlers threw at each other didn't land with *that* much force. There is no way they could have survived if they had really struck each other the way they pretended to. Oh, there would be some aches and maybe some bruises. The cuts they inflicted on themselves when they bladed would take a few days to heal. But after a good night's rest, they would be ready to put on another show, in another arena, in another city. That's the nature of the wrestling business.

After both wrestlers exited the ring, the steel cage was hoisted back up to the ceiling.

Before introducing the final match of the night, Dan Greenberg thanked the fans for attending *The Final Stand*. He invited everyone to tune in to *Monday Night Mayhem*, which would be airing the following night on TV.

I wished my mom would hurry back.

My father's match was next.

CHAPTER NINETEEN

Following a brief intermission, Prince Romulus's entrance music began to play. It was a unique mixture of tambourines, drums, oboes, and electric guitars. The Prince, accompanied by Il Gran Mephisto, ambled down the aisle, amid a chorus of boos. The Prince climbed through the ropes and stood in the center of the ring, his arms crossed, his head held high with pride and defiance. He wore a magnificent, ankle-length, purple satin robe with rows of gold sequins along the front and back. Underneath he wore purple spandex tights with PRINCE embroidered in gold lettering on the outside of one leg and ROMULUS on the other. A specially made purple headgear covered the sides of his head. The front of it was lined with imitation jewels: rubies, diamonds, emeralds, and sapphires. A tuft of curly, dark-brown hair protruded from the top. Prince Romulus projected every bit the royal image of his ring name. Mephisto, dressed in a black Armani suit with a black shirt and tie, paced around the outside of the ring, yelling at the fans, purposely riling them in true wrestling heel fashion. No one does a better job at antagonizing the audience than Il Gran Mephisto. He's a master at it.

As the Prince's music died out, the bright lights faded, replaced by dark blue ones. The familiar, spectral organ music resounded loudly. A booming explosion, detonated by the pyrotechnics crew, shook the whole auditorium.

Streams of fire blasted up from each side of the stage entrance, followed by a huge, wafting cloud of smoke.

Suddenly, there he stood—my father, the Angel of Death.

The fans jumped to their feet the moment the lights went out. Now they were rabid with excitement.

"Death! Death! Death! Death!"

"Aaagghh!" bellowed my father as he extended his scythe high in the air.

Amid the throngs of people who lined the walkway to the ring, I spotted my mom. She jostled her way along the security wall that is set up to separate the fans from the wrestlers. She stood at the very front and yelled at the top of her lungs, "Mark, I love you!"

I think she startled my father. He stopped in mid-howl and stared at her with a surprised look on his face. He quickly recovered and let out another roar. She responded by blowing him a kiss.

As he climbed into the squared circle, my mom hurried up the steps toward me. She was laughing. "Do you think I embarrassed your father?"

"Are you kidding?" I said. "No way. This is wrestling."

The organ music played itself out. The arena was relit with white lights.

The two men stood in the middle of the ring, face to face, separated only by the official in charge.

The Angel of Death fixed his dark eyes deeply into the Prince's, hypnotizing him with his snake-like stare.

"Don't look into his eyes! Don't look into his eyes!" Il Gran Mephisto screeched from outside the ring, furiously pounding on the ring apron. "Turn away, Prince! Look the other way!"

Prince Romulus snapped out of his trance just in time. He turned his head and focused his eyes on his manager. The pasty, white skull of the Angel of Death grinned devilishly.

Rocky Davis went over the rules with both men. He then instructed them to return to their corners until the bell sounded. As soon as the Angel of Death turned his back, the Prince sneaked up from behind and attacked him. Their match had begun.

CHAPTER TWENTY

Whap! Whap! Whap! Prince Romulus's fists savagely pounded the Angel of Death's back. Weakening him, the Prince grabbed him by an arm and swung him against the ropes. But the Angel of Death bounced back with a thunderous clothesline that sent Prince Romulus flying into the air before he crashed down on the mat with a loud thud.

"Yeeeah!" roared the partisan crowd. "Get 'im!"

Il Gran Mephisto immediately slid into the ring and pulled his nephew out to safety. While the Prince cleared his head, the Angel of Death turned to the crowd. With a fiery look in his eyes, he pounded his chest wildly. "Aaagghh!"

The fans ate it up. "Death! Death! Death! Death!"

Prince Romulus tried to climb back into the ring, but each time he did, the Angel of Death tossed him back out. Finally Mephisto leaped up on the ring apron just outside the ropes. The Angel of Death reached out to grab him. As he did, the Prince, still on the floor, yanked the Angel of Death by the ankles and dragged him out. Both men battled each other until the referee separated them and ordered them back into the ring.

My heart palpitated with excitement as I watched the action. The man in black with the sinister-looking skeleton face, who was pummeling his opponent with vicious chops and punches, was the same person who used to

carry me on his shoulders when I was little. He read to me
before I went to bed. He wrote poetry and love songs for
my mom. He played the guitar and the piano. And after
tonight, he would spend the next few weeks at home with
us. But at the moment, he was the Angel of Death, the
emissary from the Netherworld, sent by the Dark Forces
to destroy his enemy.

Prince Romulus gained the upper hand with two fore-
arms to the face, a standing drop kick, and a suplex.
While the Angel of Death lay face down on the mat, the
Prince climbed on his back and firmly clamped his finishing hold on him, the dreaded Procrustes Stretch.
Pinning his arms behind him, he pulled the Angel of
Death's head back, bending him backwards. It was a submission hold the Prince used to make his opponents tap
out. But of course, there was no way the Angel of Death
was going to give up. Not because he was strong enough
to withstand his painful predicament. Not because he
was able to summon the Dark Forces to energize him
with supernatural strength. Simply put, it wasn't scripted
for him to tap out.

After several agonizing moments, the Angel of Death
out-powered the Prince and broke out of the Procrustes
Stretch. He lifted the Prince over his head, then slammed
his body hard over his knee with a brutal backbreaker.
Next he went for his own finishing maneuver, the Death
Drop Pile Driver.

Once again, Il Gran Mephisto jumped up on the ring
apron in protest of what was happening to his nephew.
The Angel of Death, distracted, released the Prince without finishing him off. He seized Mephisto and dragged
him into the ring. The Prince recovered in time and man-

aged to rescue his uncle from the hands of the Angel of Death.

The fighting continued for about eighteen minutes with both men putting on a spectacular performance. And the fans loved every minute of it.

Finally, while the Angel of Death had the Prince pinned against the corner with his fingers gripped, vice-like, around his neck, the referee leaned in close to both men. I saw his lips mouth something that looked like: "Let's take it home, boys."

The wrestlers understood.

The Angel of Death flung the Prince to the ropes. As he rebounded, he whacked him with a clothesline, knocking him down to the mat. With cat-like speed, he scrambled up the turnbuckles. He spun around and readied himself to deliver an elbow drop to the defenseless Prince.

He coiled his body and sprang from the top of the ropes. But his boot slipped on the slick turnbuckle cover as he jumped. Off balance, he landed, full force, on his right ankle. His foot folded from the pressure of his weight.

"Aaahhh!" he screamed. It wasn't his trademark Angel of Death roar, but one of genuine pain.

"Mom, Dad's hurt!" I cried, jumping out of my seat.

She smiled condescendingly. "He's fine, Jesse. It's just part of the show. You know that."

"No, it's not!" I watched in revulsion as my father reeled on the floor in agony. "Look at him, he's hurt."

Rocky Davis rushed to my father's side. I could tell that he was asking him if he was all right. Prince Romulus rose to his feet, wondering what had happened. When he saw my father on the mat with the referee kneeling next to him, it didn't take long to surmise that something had gone wrong.

With twenty thousand fans watching in the arena and millions more watching from their television sets across the country, the Angel of Death knew he had to keep the show going. The Prince strutted arrogantly around the ring and yelled at the fans. They, in turn, booed and jeered. Il Gran Mephisto jumped in and raised his nephew's arm in victory.

The Prince headed over to my father and half-heartedly stomped him on the chest a couple of times. I knew he was really checking to see how badly hurt my father was. The referee ordered him back, threatening to disqualify him. The Prince retreated to Mephisto and whispered something about the situation at hand.

Rocky Davis tried to help my father sit up, but it was no use. He lay on the mat, gritting his teeth, trying desperately not to cry out.

"Dad's really hurt, Mom!" I said again. "It wasn't supposed to happen this way."

"Jesse, why are you getting yourself so worked up?" asked my mom. "Dad told us he was going to pretend to get injured during the match."

"Yeah, but not like this. He was supposed to get burned by Mephisto, remember? Look at his foot! I–I think it's broken."

His boot lay twisted to the side, limp and lifeless, like the foot on a marionette.

The crowd was screaming for the Angel of Death to get up.

"Death! Death! Death! Death!"

"Death! Death! Death! Death!"

The noise was deafening.

My father rested his head against the bottom turn-buckle trying not to move his leg. Prince Romulus was at a complete loss as to what to do next. Rocky Davis pressed his hand against his earpiece, anxiously waiting for instructions from the back.

"Death! Death! Death! Death!"

My mom, oblivious to what was happening, cheerfully clapped and joined the chorus. "Death! Death! Death! Death!" she chanted.

I couldn't contain myself any longer. I had to do something. Without thinking, I ran down to the ring.

"Dad!" I cried as I reached the security wall at ringside.

My father gazed down at me, his skeleton face crumpled in misery.

I scaled the security wall and jumped over. I didn't get more than a few feet past it before a huge pair of hairy hands nabbed me by the collar of my windbreaker and yanked me backwards. A man in a yellow golf shirt with big black letters reading SECURITY across the back held me tightly against the railing.

"Where do you think you're going, kid?"

"My dad's hurt!" I struggled to get free. "That's him, the Angel of Death!" I pointed to my father who remained sprawled on the mat.

"Yeah, sure," the security guard said with a snarl. "Get back to your seat or I'll have you thrown outta here."

"Let me go!" I tried to pull myself free from his grip, but it was no use. "Dad!"

Suddenly I was five years old all over again, trying to jump into the ring to keep my father from getting hurt. Except that this time the danger was real.

"Let him go!" I heard my mom shout from behind the security guard. "He's my son."

The security guard scowled at her. I'm sure he had no idea who she was, particularly since she had been gone most of the afternoon. He didn't recognize her face.

"Take him back to his seat, lady, and make sure he stays there, or I'll have both of you hauled outta here." He lifted me over the security wall. My mom took my arm and helped me down.

"Look at his leg, Mom!" I told her, pointing to my father. "It's broken."

She looked up at him. From her vantage point she could see that his foot seemed disjointed, almost separated from his leg. It was a sickening sight. At last she understood what I'd been trying to tell her.

"Oh, my god. Mark!" she shouted. "Mark!"

"Get back to your seats!" the security guard growled, pointing to the rows behind us. "Now!"

"But my husband's hurt," my mom tried to explain. "That's him in the ring!" She dug through her purse, searching for her backstage pass. "I'm Molly Baron. My husband is Mark Baron, the Angel of Death."

The security guard, jaded from having heard too many stories from fans who will say or do anything to get up close to see their favorite wrestlers, ignored her. He grabbed his walkie-talkie from his belt and muttered something into it. I couldn't make out what he said, but I'm sure he was calling for backup to throw us out of Madison Square Garden.

"We'd better sit down, Mom," I told her, finally regaining my composure.

Just then Prince Romulus delivered a swift kick to my father's head. He clutched his left leg and pulled him away from the corner of the ring. With great care, he flipped him over on his stomach and clamped on the Procrustes Stretch.

My father struggled for a few seconds. Then, in what wrestling fans would later call "the most stunning upset in American Championship Wrestling history," the Angel of Death tapped out. He slapped his hand on the mat several times, signaling that he was giving up. Rocky Davis called for the bell. Thankfully, the match was over.

"THE WINNER OF THE BOUT . . . AND THE NEW ACW HEAVYWEIGHT CHAMPION . . . PRINCE ROOOMULUS!" Dan Greenberg announced to the shocked and disbelieving audience.

Prince Romulus raised his hands victoriously. Il Gran Mephisto snatched the championship belt from the ringside announcers' table. He climbed into the ring and proudly buckled it around his nephew's waist.

"Booo!" yelled the angry crowd. "Booo!"

They hurled plastic cups of soda and beer at the newly crowned heavyweight champion and his uncle. The men exited the ring and hurriedly made their way to the back as debris continued to rain down on them.

The security guard completely forgot about my mom and me. He and the other guards scattered around the arena as they futilely worked to restore order. But the unhappy crowds grew rowdier and rowdier. "Booo! Booo!"

An instant later, two paramedics wheeled a gurney down to ringside. It was the gurney that had been stationed in the back that was to be used as a prop to carry the Angel of Death out after Il Gran Mephisto "burned" his face.

As the paramedics stepped into the ring and tended to my father, the near riotous crowd finally began to settle down.

Most of today's fans know that professional wrestling is a "work." Deep down, they realize that the injuries depicted in the ring aren't real. It's like watching a movie. Cops and robbers on TV shows don't really shoot each other. When the director yells "cut," the actors stop and walk away, unhurt.

Part of the fun in watching wrestling is that fans can temporarily suspend belief. For a couple of hours each week on *Monday Night Mayhem*, the Angel of Death *does* come from the darkest regions of the Netherworld. Prince Romulus *is* a member of a wealthy and powerful Italian family.

Wrestling fans can also differentiate between a staged injury and a legitimate one. Wrestlers are careful not to hurt each other. But real, often serious injuries *do* occur in the ring.

The fans at Madison Square Garden could sense that the Angel of Death was genuinely hurt. The arena grew silent. Everyone watched while the paramedics assessed the situation. After a brief examination, they lifted him from the canvas and slid him onto the gurney.

The crowd stood and applauded to show the Angel of Death that they respected his efforts at having entertained them. They wanted him to know that they hoped he was all right.

As he was wheeled past us, my mom called to him in a quavering voice. "Mark?"

My father offered a faint smile. His foot seemed to be torn off his leg, held together only by his boot. I could only imagine the pain he must be suffering.

My mom and I dashed up the stairs and headed backstage. All the way, I prayed that he would be all right.

CHAPTER TWENTY-ONE

"Where is he?" my mom cried as we shoved our way through the crowded corridor outside the first-aid room.

"Over here." Butcher Murdock took her by the arm. "But you'd better brace yourself, Molly. It doesn't look good."

A wave of fear swept over her face. She took a deep breath, held it for a moment, and then exhaled a heavy gush of air. We entered the first-aid room.

My father lay on a navy blue vinyl bed. Frank Collins, the two paramedics, and the physician in attendance, a man named Dr. Fielder, surrounded him.

The doctor had already removed my father's boot. He had to cut it away from his foot with a pair of sharp scissors. Earlier, the boot had been black. Now it was painted red with blood. From the upper part of his foot, a bone jutted out of his skin. It looked like one of those gruesome, rubber Halloween gags. Except that this was no gag.

"Oh, Mark," my mom cried. She rushed over and wrapped her arms around him.

"Hi," he whispered. He kissed her forehead. "Hello, champ."

I kept my eyes on his, avoiding looking down at his foot.

"How bad is it?" my mom asked, turning to the doctor as he worked to stop the bleeding by pressing firmly on my father's foot with a clean dressing.

"Compound ankle fracture, from the looks of things," Dr. Fielder replied without looking up. "But we won't know the extent of the injury till we get him to the hospital."

"The hospital?" said my mom.

"He'll likely need surgery," Dr. Fielder said somberly. "It's a pretty bad break."

"How long before he'll be able to wrestle again?" Frank Collins asked with concern.

The doctor shrugged. "I hope you weren't planning to use him on your show tomorrow night."

"Does it hurt a lot, Dad?" I asked. It was a stupid question, but I didn't know what else to say.

"Only when I breathe, champ," he whispered with a slight smile.

"It's getting a bit cramped in here," Dr. Fielder told us. "I'd appreciate it if you folks would wait outside until I'm done."

We stepped out of the first-aid room. One of the paramedics shut the door behind us.

"How is he?" Carlos Montoya asked. He had been standing outside the door waiting to hear the news.

"His ankle's broken," my mom said, her voice cracking. "The bone . . . pierced . . . " She swallowed, then broke into tears.

Carlos Montoya reached out and comforted her.

"Carlos, I want to ride in the ambulance with Mark," she said, brushing away her tears. "I was wondering if you could drive Jesse back to the hotel for me."

Before Carlos Montoya could answer, I exclaimed, "I don't want to stay by myself in the hotel room, Mom. I want to go with you to the hospital."

She sighed. "No, Jesse, it's very late. I'll probably be there all night."

"Your *mami*'s right," said Carlos. "Stay with my wife and me tonight, Jesse. You can sleep on the couch."

"Come on, Mom," I protested, ignoring his offer. "Let me go with you. Please? I want to be with Dad, too."

My mom's face was ashen white. Her eyes seemed to have sunk deeper into their sockets. She looked as if she had aged ten years within the last ten minutes. I wondered if my face looked as pale as hers.

This, of course, was not the first time my father had been hurt in the ring. Throughout his career, he's suffered countless injuries: a separated shoulder, a broken arm, broken fingers, broken collarbone, numerous concussions, neck injuries, tears to his knees, you name it. But this was the first time I'd been there when it happened. And seeing his bone sticking out of his bloody foot was an image I'd probably never forget.

My mom hesitated for a moment, then reluctantly agreed to let me go with her. "Thank you all the same, Carlos."

"*De nada*," he answered.

A few minutes later, the paramedics rolled my father out of the first-aid room. His leg was wrapped up and immobilized in a splint. He was still in costume and in full makeup. He looked creepy lying there dressed in black with his skeleton face paint, like a horror comic artist's portrayal of Death in a coffin.

"Hey," he whispered in a raspy voice, taking my mom's hand. "Don't worry about me. I'll be all right."

She turned to one of the paramedics. "We're riding in the ambulance with him." It wasn't a request. She wasn't asking for permission.

The paramedic turned to Dr. Fielder. The doctor nodded to show his approval.

We followed the gurney to the waiting ambulance. The paramedics lifted it, folded the wheels, and gently slid it into the back. A paramedic helped my mom in. I climbed in after her.

"I'll meet you over there," said Dr. Fielder as he shut the doors behind us. The paramedics took their places in the cab of the ambulance, flipped on the flashing lights and the siren, and we were off.

CHAPTER TWENTY-TWO

For a while we rode in silence. My father had his eyes closed. I couldn't tell if he was sleeping or if he was trying to block out the pain. Finally he spoke.

"This is it, Molly. I'm through. I can't do this any longer." His eyes were still shut. His voice was slurry. I figured the doctor had given him something for the pain.

My mom brushed back his hair from his face. It was caked with white face paint. "Don't think about that right now, Mark," she said. "Wait and see what the doctor has to say."

"No. I should've quit a long time ago." He took her hand from his forehead and kissed it. "I was stupid to have agreed to come off the top turnbuckle the way I did. I'm too old to be attempting that high-risk stuff." He paused and glanced around, taking in his surroundings. "You know, all along I'd been worried about blowing out my knee again. I never thought it'd be my ankle."

We arrived at the emergency room. Dr. Fielder pulled up behind us. He opened the rear ambulance doors, and we climbed out. The paramedics rolled my father out and wheeled him into the hospital. Dr. Fielder spoke briefly to the nurse at the admitting station. After that, my father was taken down a corridor. He and the paramedics disappeared behind two gray metal doors.

My mom filled out some forms while I sat in the waiting area.

There was a TV set hanging from the ceiling across from me. It was airing an old *I Love Lucy* episode, but I wasn't interested in watching it. A disturbing thought had been running through my head during the ambulance ride to the hospital, and I couldn't shake it loose.

Back in my old school, we read a short story called "The Monkey's Paw." It was about a soldier who had given a husband and wife a mummified monkey's paw. He claimed that the paw could grant its owner three wishes. As things turned out, the wishes did come true, but not in the way the couple expected. The husband in the story, not really believing the legend of the monkey's paw, casually wished for two hundred British pounds. Later the couple learned that their son had been killed at the factory where he worked. While the company was not assuming responsibility for the son's death, in consideration of his service, it presented the boy's parents with a certain amount of money as compensation — two hundred pounds! Later, the wife demanded that her husband wish for their son back. The man knew it was a terrible wish. The boy had died when he was caught in a machine at the factory, and his body had been badly mangled. The man realized that if he wished for their son back, he would return in that same mutilated condition. But his wife was insistent, and, ultimately, he gave in. Soon there was a sound outside their house, and the wife knew it was their dead son, risen from the grave. In the end, the man wisely wished his son back into the grave before his wife had a chance to see him.

I had forever been wishing that my father would be able to spend more time at home with us. Now, through a horrible circumstance, it appeared that he would. I'd cursed my father with a monkey's paw wish!

My head was throbbing again. It had begun to hurt when I struggled with the security guard at the arena, then it eased up. But it continued to return in spurts.

After she finished filling out the forms, my mom joined me. I nuzzled up to her. She wrapped an arm around my shoulder. Her sweater felt warm against my face, and it seemed to soothe my headache. I glanced up at the wall clock. It was almost twelve-thirty.

On TV, Lucy had gotten herself locked in a walk-in freezer. When Ricky found her, she was frozen stiff, with icicles hanging from her face. It was a funny episode, but neither one of us laughed. We sat there quietly and stared blankly at the screen.

"Mom, Dad's going to be all right, isn't he?" I asked. After seeing his foot torn the way it was, it didn't seem possible he ever could be.

She played with my hair, curling strands of it on her fingers. "Of course he is, sweetheart. I know it looks bad, and it is. But I've seen your father go through injuries like this before. He'll come out of it all right, trust me."

"Do you really think he's going to quit wrestling?"

Her fingers stopped twirling. She shifted uneasily in her chair. I sat up. She slipped her arm from my shoulders.

"Jesse, I can't tell you how many times I've wished that your father would leave the business. His being on the road so much has been a tremendous strain on all of us. When he first started wrestling, I tolerated it because I knew it was something he wanted to do. I thought he'd wrestle for a couple of years, get it out of his system, and then go into some area of law enforcement. Then he became the Annihilator. Even then, things weren't so bad because he usually wrestled in nearby arenas. And since he wore a mask, no one ever recognized him in public. We could go out and enjoy ourselves in peace. But in our wildest dreams, Jesse, neither one of us ever thought that his career would skyrocket the way it did. Now, the Angel of Death is one of the most popular sports figures in the world. There's an incredibly high demand for him, and Frank Collins is all too happy to give the public what they want."

I Love Lucy ended. It was replaced by an infomercial. A man was offering a set of eight stainless steel, dishwasher-safe steak knives for only $19.99, two more if you called right now. I wondered how many people had a need to buy steak knives in the middle of the night.

"The other day, Dad told me he wasn't going to wrestle much longer, that he was going to retire as soon as his contract expires," I said.

My mom snickered.

Immediately, I felt as if I'd said something dumb.

"Jesse, your father's been singing that song for years. Every time he gets hurt he talks about leaving wrestling."

"So, you don't think he was serious about quitting?" I asked.

"I honestly don't know." She wrapped her arm around me again, and I leaned up against her. "But watching him in the ring tonight, live, seeing how much the fans adore him, I realize that your father was born to be the Angel of Death. Destiny gave him that opportunity, and I have no right to try to take it away from him."

"But what about his foot?" I asked.

She shrugged. "It's just another injury. He'll recover from it in time. He always has. Your dad's had more work done on his body than Frankenstein's monster." She chuckled at her joke. "As soon as he gets well, I promise you he'll forget about everything he said in the ambulance. And you know what?" She sat up straight and gazed into my eyes. "I'll never again say or do anything to discourage him. If he wants to continue to wrestle, then I'll just have to learn to be more accepting of his career."

I realized that I would have to be more accepting of it, too. At least I had a father. Poor Wendell would have to grow up without his.

Some fathers were meant to be construction workers, office managers, teachers, police officers, or grocery store clerks. Mine just happened to be the black-clad, skeleton-face behemoth called the Angel of Death.

EPILOGUE

"You're not going to chicken out, are you, champ?" my father teased. We headed toward the small speed boat.

"No way." I gazed up at the sky at the huge parachutes hovering above the tropical waters of Kaanapali Beach. I'd never been parasailing, but ever since we arrived in Maui and I'd seen the flyers riding the skies, I knew at once that it was something I wanted to try. My mom was planning to videotape the whole experience. I couldn't wait to show it to Sara when we got back to San Antonio.

"Aloha!" a large, richly tanned Polynesian man warmly greeted us. He took my mom by the arm and helped her into the boat.

I took my father's cane and helped him climb aboard. I hopped in after him.

"I am Captain Kimo," said the man, "and this is my number one crew member, Afa."

His number one crew member was a muscled teenager with a tan that rivaled Captain Kimo's. I guessed he was Captain Kimo's son.

"Aloha," said Afa. He smiled broadly, exposing a gold upper front tooth. "How many will be parasailing today?"

"Just our son," my father said. "Unless he chickens out," he added, giving Afa a quick wink. He leaned his weight on his cane as he gingerly lowered himself down and sat next to my mom.

Afa squinted as he stared at my father with a hint of recognition. "Say, you wouldn't by any chance be . . . "

"My name is Mark Baron," my father said quickly, interrupting the number one crew member. "My family and I are here on vacation from San Antonio, Texas."

"Oh," said Afa, slightly embarrassed. "I thought . . . never mind." Then he muttered, "San Antonio, Texas. Home of the Alamo . . . and the San Antonio Spurs." He flashed his gold tooth once again.

Captain Kimo switched on the engine. The boat coughed a couple of times. It gave a quick jerk. Then it surged forward. A breeze sent splashes of saltwater in my face. I didn't mind, though. It felt pleasant to be cooled down from the mid-June Hawaiian sun.

Captain Kimo drove the boat about a mile and a half from shore. He stopped the boat long enough for Afa to strap the harness around my body.

"If he starts to cry, ignore him," my father jokingly told Afa.

"Waaa!" I wailed.

My mom readied the video camera.

Captain Kimo restarted the boat. As we sped away, he flipped the switch that released the cable wire to the para-sail canopy.

The line was unreeled, and I ascended to the sky. Higher and higher I soared.

Within seconds the boat below me was just a tiny speck in the water. I reached a height of eight hundred feet. I was flying!

It was an exhilarating experience to be gliding across the sky. The view was breathtaking. On one side the beach, the hotels, and the mountains made up the Maui landscape. The other side was an endless view of the turquoise-blue Pacific Ocean.

I had thought parasailing would be scary, like riding a roller coaster, but it was soothing and peaceful. I couldn't recall the last time I felt so relaxed. But then again, our whole vacation to Hawaii was that way. Even my headaches seemed to have disappeared completely.

My mom finally took me to see a doctor about them. He diagnosed them as migraine headaches that, as she had guessed, were stress induced. The doctor prescribed some medicine for them. But if we took more vacations like this one, I'd probably never have to take another pill again. My mom had suggested the trip as soon as my father was able to walk again.

He never did make an appearance at my school. Mrs. Petrosky seemed to have lost interest in inviting him after he was injured. She had wanted the Angel of Death, the "emissary from the lower regions of the Netherworld" to visit her classroom, not Mark Baron, a crippled dad of one of her students. It didn't matter. As things turned out, I developed a real love for Texas history. My grades jumped up in no time at all.

While he was still in the hospital, my father tried to submit his resignation to the ACW, but Frank Collins talked him out of it. Instead, he offered to place my father on an inactive roster. I guess he's hoping my father will change his mind about returning to the ring as soon as his ankle is 100 percent healed.

Who knows? Every time we watch *Monday Night Mayhem*, I see that sparkle in his eye. I can sense that he wishes he were there along with the boys, entertaining the fans.

For now, it's just great to have him home. My monkey's paw wish didn't appear to be a curse after all.

Afa finally began to reel me back down to the boat. My short flight to heaven was over. As I approached the boat, I could see my father flapping his arms and clucking like a chicken. My mom was having difficulty steadying the video camera, she was laughing so hard.

Maybe my trip to heaven isn't over, I thought.

Maybe it's just beginning.

Ray Villareal was born in Dallas, Texas, where he lives with his wife Sylvia and their children, Mateo and Ana. He graduated from Southern Methodist University and currently works as a reading coach for the Dallas Independent School District. Ray has written and directed numerous children's plays. *My Father, the Angel of Death* is his first book.